The Yawning Rabbit River Chronicle

Other Books by J. L. Kimmel

The Magic Gown
written and illustrated by J. L. Kimmel

L'Irresistibile Richiamo Dell'Acciuga
(The Irresistible Call of the Anchovy)
written by David Ceccarelli and J. L. Kimmel
illustrated by David Ceccarelli

The YAWNING

ЯABBIT RIVER

CHRONICLE

J. L. Kimmel • David Ceccarelli
Illustrated by David Ceccarelli

SPRING TREE
PRESS

Copyright © 2012
by J. L. Kimmel and David Ceccarelli

Cover art and design by David Ceccarelli
Cover completion by Jane Hagaman
Interior design by Jane Hagaman
Design consultant: Poppie van Herwerden
Edited by M. Leonard Baker, Caryle Duffy, Tania Seymour

Production services provided by Quartet Books

Spring Tree Press
P.O. Box 461
Atlantic Highlands, NJ 07716
www.springtreepress.com
732-872-8002

If you are unable to order this book from your local
bookseller, you may order directly from the publisher.

Library of Congress Control Number: 2012906859

ISBN 978-0-9785007-1-9

10 9 8 7 6 5 4 3 2 1

Printed on acid-free, 100% recycled paper
in the United States

*For the little rabbit hero
who crossed the road that night.*

Contents

Part I

The Rabbit Thief

Chapter One

A Troubled Forest

A long, long time ago in a troubled forest, the animals were suffering. For as many years as any of them could remember, there had been no life-giving river running through their woodlands. Instead, they relied on catching rainwater and using the groundhog's keen sense of smell to find underground springs for wells. But the rainwater was scarce, and the wells were empty now. Even the pine trees had stopped producing their nourishing cones, no longer having the strength to make them.

Each day, in their search for food and water, the animals faced dangerous trips outside the woods, where hunters with bows and arrows, crushing metal traps, and sharp hunting knives waited for them, often with tragic and deadly consequences. The evil hunters had even trained their vicious, man-like wolf creatures, called molfs, to venture into the woods and track down the most vulnerable of the animals: the babies, the elderly, and the sick. It was truly a dark time for the animals in the dying forest.

One desperate night, the animals had a meeting in a small clearing at the center of the woods. They gathered together and sat on the low, encircling stone wall that had been built long ago. In the old days, soft, thick, green moss used to cover the stones like pillows but not anymore. There was no comforting fire to sit by either, because the lack of water made fire a dangerous thing. Then, too, the fire's light could easily be seen through the thinning trees and draw the attention of the hunters and their brutal molfs.

An old graying raccoon, called "Grandpa" by everyone, slowly stood up and moved to the center of the circle to speak. "Maybe some of us need to move out of the forest for good. There just isn't enough rainwater; the summer has been so dry. Grandma and I have discussed this. We'll go. We're old. Let the young stay and try to . . . ack, ack, uuuh, ack, uuuh . . ." He began to cough hard, clutching his chest. Grandma Raccoon got up and helped him back to his seat.

"How would we decide who else should leave?" called Jimmy the squirrel from a tree limb above.

Several brown bears were huddled together, talking among themselves. Finn, the smallest bear, who had only one ear since losing the other one to a hunter's knife the previous winter, spoke up. "Anyone who's tried to leave hasn't done so well; it's a death sentence! I think we should all stay."

"I agree," said Jimmy. The animals murmured in agreement.

Just then they heard the crunching sounds of dried leaves underfoot.

"Who's there?" the one-eared bear called out.

Into the clearing stumbled Meeka, her head hanging down. She was one of the last of the few wild horses still to be found in the nearby valley. Her front legs were bloody and she wobbled from side to side, for she was badly wounded. "Mercury fell, caught in their traps hidden in the grass!" she exclaimed breathlessly. "He was trying to get me clover. They tied him up and pulled him down to the ground and beat him. The molfs attacked my legs when I tried to help. The hunters came at me with their knives, but I ran from them. There was nothing . . ." Her pitiful voice trailed off as her two front legs collapsed beneath her, and she fell to the ground.

Finn, who more than anyone in the forest was most like a doctor, came to her aid, bringing her a precious sip of water in a wooden bucket. Then he tended to her leg wounds. Finn always carried a little medical bag filled with roots and herbs that he collected from the woods.

"Oh, poor, poor Mercury," muttered Gwen, a feeble mole. "These eyes have seen the horrors of the hunters and their molfs." Gwen was practically blind. She wore thick glasses and carried a tiny cane made from a twig. "Never can you trust those beasts; they tear you apart and eat you! All the while, they are smiling . . . without any remorse . . . like ugly-faced monsters."

Gwen cried inconsolably, remembering the time when her mole family was massacred. "When they bite you, if you get away, like I did, they'll find you sooner or later. If the molfs taste your blood, even just once, they'll know where you are, even if you try to hide from them. There's no safe place anymore. No peace. Oh, poor, poor Mercury . . ."

"Shhhhh, Gwen," Finn said, trying to quiet the mole's tearful ranting before Meeka became even more upset.

Mercury was the pride of the animals. Over the years, he had gained the respect of all the inhabitants of the forest for his courage and character. The voices of his ancestors, who once flourished and freely roamed the green hills, were carried in the wind that blew back his striking black-and-white mane and tail. He was a tall, magnificent looking, black horse with large, bright white patches on his body and a white stripe like a lightning bolt down the center of his handsome black face. In his dark eyes, the fire and strength of his spirit were evident.

Meeka was a small, graceful, honey-colored mare with a golden yellow- and brown-streaked mane and tail. Her soulful brown eyes showed not only the depth of her kindness but also, most of all, her love for Mercury. With so little to eat and drink, it was doubtful she would live. After drinking some more water from the bucket, Meeka was rising slowly to her feet just as a small voice shouted out from the dark silence of the woods.

"I have a plan!" they all heard, as a tan, scrawny jackrabbit with small eyes and long, scruffy, tattered ears stepped into the clearing. It was Sean.

"You? You have a plan?" erupted Edward, a broken-winged eagle permanently injured by an arrow two winters before. "I may not be able to fly, but my talons are strong enough to break your stinkin' rabbit thief neck!"

"I have a plan to bring the river here," the rabbit insisted.

"You're a thief and a fool, Sean!" someone called out.

"You stole my honey," snarled Finn. "I know it was you."

"Me?" shrugged the rabbit.

"Yes, you! You may be the fastest in these woods, so fast even your own shadow can't catch you, but—"

"Precisely!" snapped Sean. "I have a plan to race Violet, the river goddess, and win. Then I'll bring the river back here." He slipped a worn red sack off his shoulder and took out an old green book.

"Humph!" exclaimed Carol the owl, who was the forest's librarian. "That is the oldest book in the library, and it is very special. How did you get it?"

"Oh, I just borrowed it. I was gonna return it once I was finished, but it's strange . . . my paws tingled when I picked it up."

"Oh, sure, just like you were going to return the acorns and chestnuts you stole from me!" said Jimmy the squirrel.

"And the eggs from my nest!" a mother finch cried.

"I told you, Sean, this is a special book, like no other. You shouldn't be handling it," Carol warned him.

"Nobody wants your help, Sean," said the eagle, moving dangerously close to the rabbit.

Sean quickly opened the book. "I can find her. I can find Violet, the river goddess, and bring her here!"

"You're nuts!" blurted Jimmy.

"It's just a myth, Sean," said Carol, "a story the old folks told at night around the fires. And anyway, do you know how long ago Violet . . ." Carol stopped herself mid-sentence.

"What are you going to do Sean, steal the river?" mocked the badger. "There is no river! Isn't that obvious? Not one bird has ever seen such a river, even when they could fly. Right, Edward?"

The eagle sadly nodded his head in agreement.

Meeka slowly walked across the clearing toward the rabbit and nuzzled the book with her nose. "What does it say?" Her sweet voice floated into the night air like a perfect melody and into Sean's ears.

"Tha . . . tha . . . that . . . tha . . ." Sean was stuttering.

". . . that a long time ago," picked up Carol the owl, "beyond the Valley of Giants, when there were giants, there was a beautiful river, and the river goddess named Violet watched over it. She took the shape of a deer by day and then returned to her river at night."

You could have heard a pin drop, it was so quiet. The animals were listening, wide-eyed; even the crickets held their chirping as she continued.

"Each morning, when the sun rose, a hunter would wait for her. He could not kill her because he had fallen in love and wished to be with her. But that was impossible, for he was not a god; he was a man. His name was Daniel. At night, he would lie near the river listening to her rippling sounds, and sometimes he would swim and bathe in the river by moonlight just to be close to her. The goddess had fallen in love with him, as well, and chose to be near him all day when she was a deer."

The animals sat frozen in silence. No one could speak for several minutes.

"It's just a myth," Carol the owl assured them. "Nothing true about it. The library is filled with books about these kinds of things: made-up stories."

No one else spoke. It felt like an unbreakable silence until Sean hopped in the air and shouted out, "I can find the river and the goddess!"

"What's in it for you?" Edward the eagle asked sarcastically.

"Nothing," Sean responded, looking down at his hind paws. "It's just that I can do this."

He unfolded a piece of paper, revealing a map he had drawn. "I am going to challenge the river goddess to a race to these woods, and when she follows me, I have a trick in store for her. Since she doesn't know these woods like I do, I'll win and get the river. You'll see."

"Ah, I knew it! Then the river will be yours!" exploded Edward.

"No, no! I mean it will be for the forest, for all of us."

Angrily, Edward spoke up again. "You're a thief, a criminal, and you have been your whole darn life. Good for nothing. And you believe this tale? What a fool you are!" He clasped his sharp talons around the rabbit's neck and lifted Sean off the ground.

"Let the rabbit go, Edward," commanded Grandpa, "unless you have a better plan. There's been enough suffering here already."

"You're actually gonna believe this runt?" demanded Edward.

"We're all dying, Edward; can't you see that?" replied Grandpa, wearily.

Could Sean really do this, they all wondered to themselves: a scrawny rabbit thief racing a river goddess—and winning?

"This is unbelievable. You're all crazy!" The eagle unclamped his talons, and the rabbit fell to the ground. "He's got you crazy!"

"Yes, yes, just think," said Sean, jumping to his feet and brushing off his fur. "We'll have fresh, clear, river water running over rocks covered with soft green moss, and delicious sweet clover, and crisp red autumn apples. And flowers," he promised Meeka, but she was despondent, staring off into the night.

"And all the chestnuts, walnuts, and hazelnuts you could eat, Jimmy, and the bees will return to make honey, Finn! Oh, and pinecones and fires at night to get warm by, Grandpa!" he assured them.

Sean didn't know what he could promise Edward, a cranky broken eagle who had never liked Sean anyway. The rabbit gave the book back to Carol the owl. It was the first thing he had ever returned to anyone.

"When will you go?" asked Finn.

"Tonight. Now!" he responded.

"Good luck, Sean," Carol said.

"Good luck, Sean," everyone else but Edward called out.

But no one was really very hopeful that Sean's plan would work. Even though he was a remarkably fast runner, it was doubtful he would even make it past the hunters and their molfs. Plus, wasn't this just a story from a book? Could the river goddess Violet really exist? The rabbit thief was determined to prove that she did, and for this it was difficult not to admire him, even if he was a thief.

"I'll return with the river; you'll see," he told Meeka. "I promise you." And with that the rabbit thief disappeared into the dark woods. With him, in his sack, he carried his folded map and a small supply of stolen food.

Soon Sean stood at the edge of the forest. With no time to waste, he took off with his usual lightning speed. His shadow in the moonlight struggled to keep up with him. This was something he found very amusing, like a friend to play with . . . his only friend, really. Moving quietly, careful not to end up with a leg or paw crushed in the sharp metal teeth of a hunter's trap, he made it to the high grasses in the field where Mercury had been captured just that day.

Molfs barked in the distance; the scent of rabbit was in the air! Sean heard the whistling sound of an arrow right over his head, just missing him. This was not a good place to linger, and he was off again. According to his map and notes from the book, he was to head north. With no compass, just his rabbit instincts and clever thief qualities to guide him, he went onward. And although he had considered himself unlucky all of his life—he was an orphan with no family except for the one he dreamed about—Sean figured that somehow, miraculously, he would get a sign along the way that would lead him to the river goddess. He simply had to believe that.

Chapter Two

Waiting for Rabbit News

Except for Edward, the animals in the forest sat together for most of the night after Sean left. Living so long with nothing but dismal news, they hadn't had something to hope for in a long time, and nobody wanted to break the spell of the moment. Unfortunately, Meeka's condition had been weakened by her wounds and the tragedy of Mercury's capture, so with encouragement, she lay down by the bears and closed her eyes.

Edward had disappeared into the woods but hadn't gone far, just enough for them to think he was gone; even he didn't want to be completely alone tonight. He had not been himself since he had been injured by the hunter's arrow, and he had become difficult and argumentative. It was hard for a proud eagle to no longer be able to fly, to no longer be useful as an important bird, who could soar the highest to see where the hunters were or to search for water and food.

In the past, he would have been the one to search for Mercury, but now there was no one. The animals could only imagine the worst for the stallion, as that's what had happened to other captured wild horses. Now Mercury was in the hands of the cruel hunters, wounded and mistreated. Their only hope was that he could escape alive, for if not, he would be beaten to break his spirit. But in Mercury's case, if the fire and strength of his spirit seemed to have disappeared from his eyes, it was only to fool the hunters; they would have to kill him to truly destroy his spirit.

Breaking the prolonged silence that had befallen them after Sean's departure, Jimmy spoke from a branch above. "Read to us, Carol; read to us from that special book about Violet." He secretly wanted to believe the river goddess story. He wanted to hear how beautiful the river was, the river that maybe that crazy rabbit thief really could bring back to them.

There was just enough starlight for Carol to make out the words, and she began to read from the beginning of the green book. No one knew where it had come from or who the author was.

A long time ago, in a northern land more beautiful than you can imagine—the kind of place that feels more like home than anywhere else—there was a spectacular lake at the bottom of a streaming waterfall. Surrounding the lake was a valley ringed by steep, sloping, green mountains, and through this valley of thick pine and hardwood forests ran a clear, bubbling river. All around it, the luscious green grass, moss, clover, and wild violets grew, covering the cool, smooth, gray rocks, the ground, the tree trunks, and the mountains. Almost every kind of flower, bird, bee, and butterfly, as well as many different animals, thrived happily together in this wondrous place.

It was the work of the river goddess, Violet, who watched over this land as if it were a precious treasure . . . as it truly was. By daylight, she looked after her river by taking the shape of a deer, one of her most beloved animals."

Carol paused, remembering how long it had been since deer lived in the troubled forest. They had all been killed by the hunters. Choking back the tears from her huge round eyes, she continued.

By night, Violet would enter the river and become the river goddess herself.

To the west, in Moran, a distant land near the Great Ocean in the Kingdom of Teru, a young man named Daniel, the son of King Moran, had gone away, preferring to follow his dream of being a great explorer rather than wait to become king someday. With his bow and arrow, he wandered into the vast Zusia Mountain Range and trekked over the high snowy passes. From there, he ventured into the misty lands and walked for weeks, until one day he came upon the unusual Echo Valley.

Every night there, as he lay under a brilliant blanket of glistening stars, a wind would stir. In the wind, he heard mysterious whispers of a word, as if it were a clue or a warning. The word was "Violet," and here, in this echoing place where the wind talked, Daniel Moran sensed that by continuing on he would one day understand what it meant. Something—or someone, for it felt to him more a name than a flower—had begun to inhabit his mind and heart. So he moved on toward the northeast, following the calling of Violet in the wind.

"Uh, I wonder if Sean can hear the wind talking, too?" interrupted Gwen the mole. "Oh, I wonder. Oh, I hope so. Violet, Violet, help us!" the little mole called out.

"Shhhhh, Gwen. Quiet down." Finn demanded. "Please, keep reading, Carol."

"Okay, if you all want me to?" Carol questioned.

"Yes!" they all replied in one voice.

Carol was secretly happy to continue, because now it was coming to the exciting part.

In time, Daniel came to a green valley once populated by giants, who had made a passageway through a mountain. It was here, by a stroke of luck, that Daniel happened to notice a lone rat scurrying toward the opening of the tunnel, seemingly with purpose—

"Rats are very smart, you know," interrupted Gwen.

"Yes, yes, we know, Gwen," said Finn. "Then what happened, Carol?"

Daniel followed the rat for hours, moving quickly through the tunnel.

"Maybe the rat was helping Daniel," interjected Gwen.

"Gwen, please, we're listening to Carol!" the badger called out.

Patiently, like a good storyteller, Carol began again.

Daniel was led to Violet's own beloved forest on the other side of the mountain. When Daniel looked around, the rat had disappeared into the thick grasses and was not seen again.

"Ahhhh, he found her!" exclaimed Grandma Raccoon, in excited suspense at the thought.

"Well, not exactly yet," commented Carol, before continuing.

It was not long before Daniel unwittingly caught sight of Violet, not as a beautiful woman but as the exquisite deer whose form she assumed during daylight hours. A skilled hunter—and not knowing that his quest for food was leading him to stalk the very object of his affection—Daniel deftly tracked his prey through the woods and along the riverbank, waiting to make his move.

Silently, he took an arrow, placed it in the bow and drew back. He aimed. From a tree above, a robin sang. The arrow flew into the air but missed.

"Oh, thank goodness!" blurted out Jimmy from the branch, to which the rest of the animals nodded their heads in agreement. "Then what happened, Carol?" the squirrel wanted to know.

"Well, the deer ran away and disappeared into the forest," Carol told them.

Like a spell had been cast upon him, Daniel's visit in the woods seemed to take a turn for the worse. Although his pursuit of the dreamlike Violet made him believe that he should continue on with the journey, he couldn't seem to leave the woodlands. Every time Daniel tried, he discovered that it was impossible. Deprived of his usual excellent sense of direction, no matter which way he went, he would find himself lost. Finally, it occurred to him that he must be in an enchanted forest, and if he were not careful, his life would never be the same again. But of course, it was already much too late for that!

His first strange encounter was along a path filled with rain puddles. He came to a crossroad where "puddle fairies" lived, the so-called "little black eyes." They were waiting for him to get him lost, hopefully for a long time—maybe even forever—for they didn't care much for visitors with bows and arrows.

"Ah, me either!" declared Finn. All the other animals were silent, like in a trance . . . just listening.

"Me, too," agreed Carol and kept reading.

These were mischievous little water-fairy creatures that looked kind of like tiny, thin mermaids with long grass hair and small black eyes. They were about the size of a penny and were all shades of green.

During the day, little black eyes were found along the paths—always at crossing points—swimming and splashing in the rainwater puddles and waiting for anyone they didn't like, which was pretty much everyone, to go by. Incredibly patient creatures, they could wait a hundred years or more for someone to come strolling their way. Then they would whisper which way to go . . . always telling the wrong way, always trying to get someone lost. And there were visitors who were lost forever because of them!"

Where'd the visitors go?" inquired Jimmy.

"They just eventually perished, probably," answered Grandpa raccoon.

"Oh," Jimmy responded; then Carol continued.

At night, the puddle fairies would roll up into little balls and regret their very bad behavior, but if given a chance to do it all over again to any passerby the next day, they would. They were always regretful at night but never the next day!

There were several chuckles heard in the group at the idea of such naughty fairies.

"We need some little black eyes here to get the hunters and the molfs lost forever!" said Gwen, excitedly.

"Yes, but we have no rain puddles, Gwen," said Jimmy.

"Oh, that's true," Gwen answered, weakly. "I hadn't thought of that."

"And listen to this," Carol said.

Little black eyes had no predators because they were poisonous, and nothing could eat them.

"Uh, not like us; we get eaten," Gwen whimpered to herself.

All the other animals were quiet, imagining this strange but amazing water creature in this strange but amazing place with rain puddles and a river goddess.

Carol gave them a few minutes to ponder the tale, then began reading again.

Daniel's next strange meeting was with another kind of impish and cantankerous creature, the "lumps," or "grass goblins," in the fields, which were loaded with them. At first he didn't see anything, for they lived under the soft small mounds of earth that had long, thin, green- and straw-colored grass growing from the tops. That was really their hair. The mounds were an inviting place to rest your head or sit. The grass goblins weren't very tall and varied from ankle high to knee high to hip high. They were all shades of green, from light celery to dark spinach, and they didn't eat food: they just drank all the rainwater they could. They loved to take someone's food, however, and just taste it, then spit it out. Stepping on one guaranteed being tripped or pinched; lying on one would get your hair pulled or your cheek bitten, if they could get a good hold on you. Still, mostly the grass goblins preferred to have nothing to do with anyone unless provoked or stepped on.

It seemed as if a whole year went by as Daniel wandered in the woods. Then, one warm evening as he lay in the grasses near the river, enchanted by the sound of the moving water and the scent of lilacs, he saw Violet—as the deer—again. He lay perfectly still, quiet as a mouse. His bow was in the grass, out of reach. He'd wait until the deer moved down to the river, he thought; then he could retrieve his weapon and try to get another shot at it.

The hours passed, and the darkness of night was descending upon the land. In the twilight, as if it were a dream right before his eyes, the deer moved slowly into the water as if to cross the river. But instead of crossing, the deer disappeared into the darkening liquid. Then, a watery nymph emerged which morphed into a goddess with human-like form. Adorned with blossoms and wild violet flowers, she wore a flowing dress of different shades of blue and green, velvety and smooth. Her eyes were the green of moss, and her long dark hair was the color of the soil of the river bottom. Daniel stared in rapt amazement at the most beautiful young woman he (or anyone else, for that matter) had ever seen: Violet, the river goddess.

Carol looked up. All eyes were on her; everyone was listening intently. Even Edward had moved back closer to the group so as not to miss a word. Only Meeka, still sleeping restlessly near Finn and the rest of the bears, was not breathlessly awaiting the rest of the story.

"Please keep reading, Carol," Finn implored, voicing what everyone was thinking.

"Do you think Sean found her yet?" an excited Jimmy the squirrel asked.

"Don't be ridiculous, Jimmy; he's not that fast," replied a captivated Edward. "Let's hear more."

"Okay then," answered Carol, with some hesitation.

The gaze of Violet, the river goddess, fell upon Daniel like starlight on the water's surface. From that moment on, he loved her. He loved her as the deer by day and as the young woman she was at night. He was close to her always, as she was to him, for Violet had fallen in love with the man. He was no longer a hunter; he couldn't kill anything so beautiful in a forest so beautiful.

Carol tried to hold back the tears, but she couldn't; a forest so beautiful, where nothing could be killed, was too hard to

think about with all this sadness surrounding them every day. She closed the book. She just couldn't tell them the rest of the story right now; she would keep that to herself for the time being. Meeka was taking short heavy breaths now. Finn sat close by her side, stroking her head.

In their own private silence, everyone was thinking about Sean, the rabbit thief—even the cranky Edward.

Chapter Three

The Great Watcher

All through that night, by the light of the stars and a waxing half moon, Sean had traveled north at his usual fast rabbit pace away from the troubled forest he knew as home. It was now nearly dawn.

Whack! Sean stumbled to the ground. He had tripped on something hard and sharp. He rubbed his front right leg. He was wounded but not terribly.

"Ugh! What is this place?" he said out loud, seeing that he was lying in a pile of bloody skulls, spines, and leg bones. It smelled awful, like rotting flesh. Adjusting to the light, Sean saw dead sheep carcasses lying all around him.

"You better get out of here!" called a voice.

"Shut up, Ollabell! Shut up!" another said sharply but in a lower voice.

The rabbit stood up and straightened the bag across his shoulder. Looking into a cluster of tall pine trees, he tried to make out where the voices were coming from. He noticed something white, like a sheep, tied to one of the tree trunks.

"Did you say that?" Sean asked the animal. The sheep stood motionless and silent.

"Shhhhh! It will hear you," was whispered from above, where pinecones dangled from the trees, swaying back and forth.

"Tell him, Stan, tell him; tell him about the monster," the voice said from a branch above Sean. A pine head was talking.

Pine heads were pinecone-like creatures that hung from the pine trees. They looked almost like regular pinecones, but the top half was the head. They hung from the branches using large hands that were attached to long skinny arms that looked like stems.

Ollabell was a talkative, round, female pine head, and Stan was a thinner, more serious, quiet male one.

"Tell me about the monster," Sean called to them. The rabbit picked up a rock and threw it, missing them on purpose.

"Stan, he is throwing rocks at us!"

"You did it now, Ollabell!"

Sean threw another rock, a bigger one, hitting the branch they were hanging from. It shook hard enough that the two pine heads fell to the ground.

"What are you?" Sean asked, picking them up.

"Pine heads," they both answered at the same time.

"And what's this monster you're talking about?" Sean demanded.

Before either of the pine heads could reply, Sean heard crunching nearby.

The sheep moved nervously, pulling at the rope. "Baa! Baa! Baa!" it bleated piteously.

The pine heads trembled.

From the woods, a rogue molf was swiftly approaching, sniffing the ground.

"It's the monster! Run!" cried Ollabell.

Sean quickly stuffed the two pine heads into his sack. He leaped toward the sheep and untied the knot of the rope with the swiftness and dexterity of an accomplished thief. With his hind legs, he gave the sheep a good, strong shove to make it run away. The molf, frenzied by the scent of rabbit, was now after Sean!

Sean sprinted along the only path there was and into a great valley. A line of light glowed from the mountainside to his left. The molf followed, biting at the air and almost getting hold of the red sack on Sean's back. Ollabell and Stan jiggled along with the stolen food.

"You shouldn't have opened your big mouth," Stan scolded Ollabell for getting them into this mess. Ollabell ignored him; she had discovered a honey cake and begun to nibble on it.

The rabbit zigzagged, rapidly changing course. He scrambled up a rocky grass slope past a flock of scattering sheep. The molf lashed out at him, but Sean jumped out of the way. Again the molf lashed out, and again the rabbit jumped, bouncing the pine heads out of the sack, but they held on!

To Sean's horror, on the other side of a large boulder there was another molf, feasting on a slaughtered sheep. The beast looked up and snarled. Close behind, the pursuing molf leaped at Sean. The rabbit hopped out of the way as if springs were in his legs but toppled right onto a wooly sheep. They all tumbled around in the grass.

Just then, the sloping mountain rumbled and shook the ground. Suddenly, from out of nowhere, the wind howled. Dirt and grass flew around in the air, sticking to Sean's fur and the sheep's thick wool coat. Then, like they were words announcing the arrival of something supernatural, the sounds of rock cracking and wood snapping became deafening. The ground started to rise, and Sean thought it was the end of the world. The pine heads retreated back inside the sack.

It was all over in less than thirty terrifying seconds. From the mountainside had risen a giant, horned sheep-man, one hundred times the size of an ordinary sheep. His matted sheep's hair was covered in dirt and grass, and he had great curved sheep horns and an amazing sheep-man face.

Stan and Ollabell peeked out of the sack. "It's the Great Watcher!" they shrieked.

The molfs cowered, frozen in place. Sean backed away as the Great Watcher blew at the molfs. Like shriveled, dried-up leaves, the beasts were blown down the side of the mountain, bouncing off rocks and yelping all the way to the bottom. They staggered away into the forest and disappeared from sight.

Eerily, like being drawn to a magnet, the sheep gathered around Sean, closing in tighter and tighter. After what he had just been through, to be crushed by sheep was not what Sean had in mind. It was time to speak up.

"Excuse me, Mister Great Watcher. I'm looking for Violet, the river goddess," he yelled out, as loudly as he could.

The sheep went strangely quiet. Any breeze there had been now became still. The sheep-man's intense black eyes looked straight at Sean.

"Not 'Mister Great Watcher,' just 'Great Watcher,'" corrected Ollabell.

Sean ignored her.

"For what reason is a rabbit looking for a river goddess?" boomed the mountain sheep-man's giant voice.

Sean was usually an exceptionally clever talker, as well as a fast thinker and master of distraction, but not now.

"Speak up, rabbit!" Stan demanded.

"I . . . I . . . I come from a troubled forest with no river," Sean stuttered. "The animals there . . . they are dying. The hunters and their molfs, like the ones who killed your sheep . . . they capture us and kill us. Our once beautiful home . . . it has become our prison. I said . . . no, I promised . . . my friends . . . I would bring the river back to them."

"Did you hear that, Ollabell?" whispered Stan. "Would you stop eating and listen to this!"

"Are you the leader or king of this troubled forest? A great warrior? A hero?" the Great Watcher inquired.

"I'm a . . . a . . . well, I'm kind of a thief, actually," Sean managed, obviously both embarrassed by and proud of this admission.

"Ahhhhhh : . . a rabbit thief has come here to steal a river from a goddess."

"Who said 'steal'? I'm going to race her for the river, fair and square!" The words exploded out of Sean's mouth at this insult to his character. He might be a thief, but he wasn't a cheat.

"But you're already injured, my little hero. That's not a good beginning when challenging a river goddess."

Sean looked down; his leg was bleeding. "It's nothing."

"Even if you found her, what would you say? You don't even speak her language. No one does anymore."

"I'll figure it out. I'll take my chances."

The Great Watcher couldn't help but admire this bold little creature. "Come closer, rabbit. What is your name?"

Squeezing out from among the sheep, the rabbit nervously moved toward the giant.

"Sean," he replied boldly, somewhat surprised at the strength of his own voice.

"Sean?" the sheep-man repeated. "Sean?" he said again. "Come even closer!" he ordered.

Sean edged closer. Ollabell and Stan hid inside the bag.

The Great Watcher pulled a weathered wooden stick out of the ground and brought it near the rabbit's tattered left ear.

There was a flash of fire, and Sean felt a burn. He rubbed his ear. Although Sean couldn't see it, the stick had made a tattoo on his ear.

"Your courage is your good fortune, Sean. Now you carry the symbol of the Great Watcher. If your heart is pure, my sheep will take you to the river goddess."

Sean didn't know what he meant by "good fortune." Nothing Sean had done was much good, so he doubted that his heart was very pure. Then, too, he was more clever than he was courageous, so . . .

The sheep-man's face leaned closer. "To be awake is to listen! To be awake is to sing! A river is heard before it is seen!"

Just then, Stan popped his head out of the sack. "Excuse me, Mister Sean, Ollabell and I, we won't be coming with you. If you could just take us back to the pine trees, we'll be fine, thank you. Or we can get out here."

Sean ignored the pine head, for he was—perhaps for the first time in his life—undoubtedly and completely speechless.

Like time had frozen, he just stood there; his rabbit feet stuck to the ground.

"Sometimes there are no words to be spoken, and silence is the best choice," the Great Watcher reassured him, like a teacher to his student or like the wise father that Sean had never known.

Just then the ground rumbled, and Sean had to move quickly, because everything else was. Sean and the pine heads looked on in amazement as the Great Watcher descended into the mountainside of grass and rock. Before long, it was all just ground again, and although not really sure why, Sean wished the giant sheep-man hadn't left.

Like a white, wooly cloud, the sheep began to move all together, with Sean caught in the middle. Surrounded, and with Ollabell and Stan still in his bag, Sean walked slowly across the sloping green mountain and onto the worn sheep path at the floor of the Valley of the Giants.

Normally, such a sheep's pace would have been as slow as molasses for the speedy Sean, but somehow it felt just right, as though everything were slowing down—perhaps because it was. Sean realized that he should have asked the Great Watcher how far he had to go to find the river goddess. He hadn't thought of that. Nowhere in the green book he had borrowed from the troubled forest's library had it mentioned exact details. He wondered how much more he didn't know.

Inside the sack, Ollabell and Stan chattered to each other about how unfortunate they were to be traveling with this rabbit thief. Still, the food was good at least.

"Let me have some of that," Sean heard coming from his sack.

"Mmmmmmmm!"

I'll bet they found Finn's honey cakes, thought Sean. The best honey cakes made. He should know. He stole them from every bear in the woods, but Finn's were the best. *He must have a secret recipe.*

Sean pulled the bag around to his front and opened it. Ollabell had a honey cake in her hand and her mouth was stuffed. He grabbed at the cake, but she held on to it with her large hands as if it were a pine tree branch. A piece broke off, and Sean ate it. *Ridiculous pine heads*, he thought.

By evening, Sean, Stan, Ollabell, and their sheep guides were near the end of the valley. Behind them, in the distance, the sun was dipping behind the Great Watcher's mountain. At the end of the valley, they came upon a vast thick forest of giant white birch trees and oaks with rich golden-orange leaves. The temperature seemed colder, and they could see their breath in the air. A light snow began to fall. Sean's eyelids suddenly felt like lead weights, and he began to yawn. He climbed up onto one of the sheep. He just needed a brief nap, he told Stan and Ollabell.

Lying on his back, not yet asleep, with the snow falling ever so lightly on his face, Sean heard low voices coming from the trees. He raised his head from the sheep's wooly coat. "Do you hear that? What is that, Stan?"

"Oh, I don't think you should tell him, Stan," whispered Ollabell.

"Can you see the trees, Sean?" said Stan, paying no attention to Ollabell's warning. "Look more closely at the trees."

Curious, Sean slipped off the sheep's back and walked closer to several huge oaks. The mystery of the disappearing giants of this valley was about to be revealed, for inside each tree trunk stood men, women, and children giants—families of them, frozen forever in wood. It was obvious that they had committed some terrible wrong of great consequence, but Sean couldn't imagine what.

Sensing Sean's unasked question, Stan spoke up. "When the giants lived in this valley, they knew that the sheep who carried the symbol of the Great Watcher were like his children, and they promised never to harm them. Now typically, the giants ate 'croggs,' delicious-tasting little animals that looked like tusked pigs with rabbit ears"—Stan interrupted his story and pointed to Sean's ears, then hastily added, "Oh, sorry!" before continuing—"and striped bodies like a tabby cat. They were plentiful in the valley and throughout the region. The croggs rooted in the ground and made tunnels, almost like ants do, and except for wild berries in the spring and cabbages and turnips in the fall, croggs were the giants' main source of food.

"Tragically, though, one night several of the giant men conspired to disregard the Great Watcher's wishes and broke their promise of never harming or eating his sheep. They thought that he would not notice if only one or two of the sheep were missing, but that was not the case. And so it happened that after the sheep were slaughtered and roasted by these few wrongdoers, all of the remaining giants were invited to partake of the feast. Being unable to resist this temptation sealed their fate, since the promise had been broken. All were doomed by the Great Watcher to spend eternity locked inside the giant trees rooted to the forest floor, condemned until the end of time to whisper through the forest winds."

"Hmm," muttered Sean, "I know of some hunters that should happen to, but in fairness, I think that's really kind of harsh of the Great Watcher. Forever is such a long time, don't you think, Stan? I mean, do you think that was a just punishment?"

Stan shrugged, for questioning the Great Watcher was a bold thing to do and possibly dangerous, and he was reluctant to do so. Maybe they would end up in a tree for just talking about it. Sean was a thief and broke the rules and took risks on a daily basis. Stan, after all, was a simple, law-abiding pine head, who hung from a pine tree. Stan had never stolen a thing in his life or done anything outside the law.

"Maybe you have a point, Sean; eternity is a very long time," Stan replied, "but perhaps we'd better not question such things."

This philosophical conversation trailed off as the whispering from the trees suddenly increased, so the rabbit and the pine heads moved away from the woods and back to the sheep.

Sean again climbed onto a sheep's back and this time drifted off to sleep. It wasn't long before he was dreaming of a beautiful river like the one described in the green book. Although he didn't even know what a running river sounded like—for there had never been one in the troubled forest in his lifetime—he thought he could hear one. It was the most beautiful sound in the world. This was the best dream Sean had ever had. "Hello? Violet? Are you there?" he called out in his sleep. "I want to race you for the river."

Stan seemed concerned. He asked Ollabell, "What's he talking about? I don't see any river, do you?"

"No, no, I don't, but these roasted chestnuts are very good," she responded.

Stan shook his head; when food was around, Ollabell could think of very little else.

The air temperature grew even colder, and now gray clouds moved in and thickened in the sky. It began to snow harder.

"I don't think the rabbit is doing very well, Ollabell," whispered Stan, looking out of the sack and stretching his long arm to feel Sean's forehead. "Do you think he has a fever? Maybe from the wound on his leg?"

"I don't think so," answered Ollabell, as she yawned and slowly fell asleep. Finally, Stan did the same. It had been a long day for the little pine heads. The herd of sheep plodded along, carrying the sleeping rabbit and pine heads while the snow continued to fall hard all night.

Chapter Four

Meeting Robert Snow

"**W**ake up, rabbit, wake up!" Stan and Ollabell were banging Sean on the head.

The snow had stopped, and the sheep were gone. Sean was on the ground, almost completely covered in snow.

"I think he's dead!" exclaimed Ollabell, poking him some more.

Sean opened his eyes and looked around, surprised. He jumped to his feet and shook himself to full awareness. "I'm awake! I'm awake!" he shouted at Stan and Ollabell. "Stop thumping on me!"

Clumps of snow fell to the ground while the pine heads, dangling like earrings, held onto Sean's big ears. Sean found himself standing next to a steep mountain wall.

"What's that?" he asked the pine heads, pointing to a symbol scratched on the wall.

"That looks like the thing on your ear," Stan commented. "Doesn't it, Ollabell?"

"Really?" said Sean. "That's very observant of you, Stan. Let's see if you're right."

Sean carefully felt the design on his ear, then traced it in the snow. Glancing back and forth intently, he compared it with the one on the wall. "Well, it's no word I know or even a familiar language." He thought of what the sheep-man had said to him: "You carry the symbol of the Great Watcher." He touched the symbol on his ear, then pushed on the symbol on the wall and ran his paw over the rock. He knocked on the rock as if it were a door, shouting "Hello!" But nothing happened. "According to the green book, there is supposed to be a tunnel here that Daniel found. I wonder where it is. I think this is the place."

Ollabell and Stan looked at each other and shook their heads in concern. They began to think that Sean was crazy.

Sitting down in the snow with his back against the mountainside, Sean dug in with his huge hind paws and pushed as hard as he could, grunting with the effort.

"What's wrong with him?" Ollabell whispered to Stan.

"I heard that, Ollabell," Sean shot back at her, straining mightily. "I guess you have to be one of those giants, or at least bigger than me." Sean gasped in disappointment. "So if I'm wearing the tattoo of the Great Watcher, what should I do?" he asked himself out loud. "Say some magic words? I don't know any." Then he remembered something else the Great Watcher had said: "Sometimes there are no words to be spoken."

"We should go back, Sean," said Stan.

"Shhhhh . . . be quiet . . . don't say a word. I'm thinking," Sean commanded and stood silently in front of the mountain. The pine heads sat on his shoulders. It was difficult for them to be quiet. They were fidgeting and whispering to each other about what curse or horrible spell they might encounter.

"Shush, you two! Be quiet as a mouse," Sean scolded. It was funny that he had said that because just then they all heard it: a bell jingling. It was hard to say where it was coming from until a silvery-gray rat with a very long curly tail ran past Sean's feet in the snow, turned toward him, and stood up on its hind legs.

"Uh, that's not a mouse, Sean. That's a rat!" Ollabell said.

"A rat with clothes," added Stan. "Very distinguished clothes."

To their astonishment, the rat wore a long black coat with pockets, a purple scarf wrapped around his neck, and a purple wool sweater with pockets. On top of his head, he had a black-and-white, felt, three-cornered hat with a green quill feather tucked in it, and on the tip of the hat sat what looked like an inkwell. In his front paws, he carried a yellow feather and a rolled-up piece of paper that looked like an official document or declaration. He even wore striped green-and-yellow socks on his hind paws. Around the rat's neck was a purple string, on which a tiny silver bell was tied.

"Aha! Daniel's rat!" Sean said. "From the green book. Are you him . . . or a relative, perhaps? You must know the way."

It was then that the rat bowed, carefully unrolled the paper, and began to read, not answering if he was or wasn't the very rat that Daniel had followed into Violet's land. Nevertheless, he seemed to be an important rat; that was certain.

"It is with great pleasure that I, Robert Snow, welcome . . . um . . . may I have your names please?"

"Sean."

"I'm Stan Pinehead, and this is Ollabell Pinehead."

"Yes, yes, I'm Ollabell Pinehead."

The rat looked at Sean. "Do you have a last name? To make this official, you must."

"No, I don't," Sean told him. "I don't know my last name."

Ollabell whispered in Sean's ear, and he nodded. "Yes, good idea, Ollabell. Call me 'Sean the Rabbit Thief,'" he told the rat.

"As you wish," said Robert Snow. "That already sounds like a legendary name." Whereupon he took his yellow feather, dipped it in the inkwell on the top of his hat, wrote on the paper, and resumed reading.

"It is with great pleasure that I, Robert Snow, welcome Sean the Rabbit Thief, Stan and Ollabell Pinehead." Then, with great ceremonial pomp and flourish, he bowed to them and continued. "Congratulations! You are the first in a very long time to find this place. You must be on a worthy journey."

Having welcomed them, the outrageously garbed rat rolled up the paper, which carried the seal of the Great Watcher, and gave it to Sean, who then gave it to Stan, who then gave it to Ollabell, who put it in the red sack.

"Thank you, but what place is this? I am looking for a tunnel that goes through the mountain, like the one Daniel Moran discovered, to find Violet the river goddess. I must find the river goddess right away," Sean said. "I have a river to win!"

The rat took something from his pocket and held it out to Sean, who accepted the much-folded piece of paper. He unfolded it and unfolded it and unfolded it and finally was able to read it out loud: "It is never easy to travel these places. Sing this."

Sean glanced up, and said, "You know, Mr. Snow, I don't really have time for these formalities."

Robert Snow just glared at Sean disdainfully, as if to say, *What you think you have time for, or don't have time for, makes no difference here.*

Obligingly, Sean began reading the words that followed:

A river runs from you to me
This river runs for eternity
A silent promise never broken
Of true love, so sweetly spoken

A heart that beats for you and me
One pure heart for eternity
A world like ours is never broken
With my song, like wings, now open!

Robert Snow shook his head disapprovingly and stepped toward Sean, handing him another multifolded note. And again, Sean continued unfolding it until he came to the words: "You must sing it!"

Sean looked at the rat and with more than a hint of impatience in his voice said, "*I am not* a singing rabbit; I'm a *thief* and a very fast *runner*, and I'm going to race the river goddess for the river and win it! Besides, I *can't* sing!"

Straightening himself up to present his most officious and formal self, Robert Snow proclaimed as loudly as a rat could:

An opening to such a place
of magic, love, and grace,
there's no such thing as a race
to find or win such a river!

A heart that sings is the only key,
a heart of courage and humility
on this matter trust in me
to find such a river!

"I think he's too shy to sing alone," said Ollabell. "Let's sing it with him, Stan. Come on, Sean, we'll sing it with you."

Sean looked at the rat, who shook his head, implying that they couldn't do that.

Robert Snow quickly handed Sean another of the folded notes, and again Sean went through the lengthy process of unfolding it. He was beginning to lose his patience with this rodent poet with so many folded-up notes. Finally, he got to the writing and read, "You must trust me. Sing!"

Sean sighed deeply and very audibly, a possible sign of res-ignation. He cleared his throat and moved about, trying to find a comfortable position. He took a deep breath, closed his small eyes briefly, then opened them to look down at the piece of paper. He began to sing in his rabbity falsetto voice.

A river runs from you to me
This river runs for eternity
A silent promise never broken
Of true love, so sweetly spoken
A heart that beats for you and me
One pure heart for eternity
A world like ours is never broken
With my song, like wings, now open!

Stan and Ollabell clapped. "That was beautiful, Sean," they both said, "just beautiful."

Sean blushed under his furry cheeks. It was the first time he had ever sung.

"Look, Sean!" shouted Ollabell, pointing to the symbol on the wall of the mountain. It was turning around in circles, like a wheel.

Obviously pleased, Robert Snow looked at Sean, then turned and approached the massive mountain wall. "Sing it again, Sean!"

This second time, the words came easier. And as Sean repeated the song, the symbol rotated a little faster, now more like a spinning pinwheel.

"Again!" shouted Robert Snow.

Sean sang it for a third time, louder and stronger now, and the symbol spun so fast it began to bore a hole in the stone wall. A gush of wind blew from the circle.

"Wow! This is amazing! Can we sing with Sean now?" Ollabell asked Robert Snow.

"Sure, why not?" replied the rat.

Whereupon Stan and Ollabell joined with Sean for the fourth singing of the song, a rousing chorus of voices in bad but lusty harmony. Magically, the opening grew bigger and bored deeper into the stone until finally, with a burst of light that blew off Robert Snow's hat, a tunnel appeared in the mountainside. It was a large passageway, big enough for two giants to walk side by side with ease.

Satisfied, the rat fixed his hat back on between his small ears, turned to Sean, Ollabell, and Stan, and exclaimed, "I bid you farewell!" Making little jingling sounds, he scurried into the tunnel . . . the tinkle of the bell becoming fainter and fainter as he disappeared into the dark.

"Robert!" Sean called out, but there was no answer. "Violet!" he called, but nothing. "I think that was her. I bet it was," declared Sean.

"Who?" asked Stan.

"Violet, the river goddess!" he proclaimed.

"The river goddess?" questioned Ollabell.

"Sean, that was a rat," said Stan. "His name was Robert Snow, not Violet."

"I know that, Stan, but a river goddess can be anything she

wants. You know, change form, play tricks," he exclaimed. "She's magic! Testing me. She has already found me. See how easy this is going to be. I'll be back to the forest with the river before anyone expects me."

"One song and he knows everything now about river goddesses," commented Ollabell.

"I don't think it was her," whispered Stan. "I think he has a fever—or something worse!"

"Maybe he's a *crazy* rabbit thief," added Ollabell.

"That's for certain," answered Stan.

"Never mind, you two; let's just go," Sean told them.

Stan and Ollabell climbed obediently into the red sack, and Sean took off into the tunnel. "Ridiculous pine heads," Sean muttered to himself.

"I heard that!" exclaimed Ollabell, exploring the contents of the sack for something to nibble on. She wondered just how long this journey was going to be and whether the food would hold out. *Ah, well, I'll worry about that later*, she thought, having discovered another delicious honey cake.

Although the only underground passage Sean had ever seen before was a rabbit hole, his keen sense of direction and sharp eyesight guided them through the tunnel. And seeing where he was going wasn't as difficult as he had imagined, thanks to a strange greenish light emanating from moss that covered the walls. Stan, who was pretty knowledgeable about plants and trees, explained to Sean that this astonishing phenomenon was known as bioluminescence, kind of like what makes fireflies glow in the night sky.

Along the way, Stan remarked to Ollabell inside the bag, "I still don't know why a rabbit thief would care enough to risk his life to find a river goddess and steal the river for a forest."

"Shhhhh . . ." whispered Ollabell, but Sean had heard them. It was a fair question; he had never really cared about much and stole whatever he needed from the other animals. But this was different. It was as if this were meant to be, as if his whole life had prepared him for just this moment. He couldn't really explain it, but he simply "knew" that he was finally in the "right place at the right time." And as scared as he was about what might lie ahead, he never even considered turning back.

He could hear Ollabell and Stan bickering over nuts and honey cake and whose fault it was that they were in this predicament. *Their company, although a little noisy at times, is actually turning out to be comforting,* Sean thought. He had become sort of fond of the pine heads, and although he would never admit it to them, he was glad they were along for what was turning out to be a remarkable journey.

After almost a full day's walk, with incredible excitement, Sean started to see green vines growing from cracks in the stone and dirt walls, and he imagined that he must be getting closer to the other side of the mountain.

"Look!" he told Stan and Ollabell. Around the next turn, they saw immense stone steps climbing upward. Ascending the stairs to an opening covered with ivy and flowering vines like a curtain, he peeked through to see a green vista unlike anything he had ever known before and a sky so blue and clear that he thought surely it must be a painting. Sunlight filtered down through the leaves like a shower of warm, dazzling, dappled light. He walked into an open field of sweet-smelling grass and clover that was moving ever so slightly in the breeze. It was just like the description in the book: "The grass was greener than any green you could imagine." Unquestionably, this had to be the world of the river goddess, Violet.

Ollabell and Stan poked their heads out of the bag and looked around, wondering if there were any pine heads in this beautiful place.

One of the first things Sean did was to find a hollowed log, something he could easily sit in. This he leaned up against the entrance to the tunnel. He was already planning how to beat the river back through to the forest. Then Sean hurried through the grass, searching for the river he knew had to be here. Several hours passed, and the light was fading. Still there was no sign or sound of a river, just the sea of never-ending green meadows and the magnificent forest of great trees. No Robert Snow either. It was as if the land were abandoned . . . empty.

That was far from true, but what lived there was hidden for now. The fields were actually teeming with "lumps," the so-called grass goblins, and they were not happy to be disturbed or walked on by any stranger to the land, even if it was a rabbit. Later that night, while resting on a mound of soft grass, Sean awoke and falsely accused the pine heads of pulling his ears. Ollabell and Stan later had a tug-of-war over a honey cake with a lump who was trying to steal their favorite treat from the bag.

That first night, a few delicate rain showers passed over, and in the morning light Sean and the pine heads drank fresh rainwater from a leaf bowl the rabbit had made. Later on, Sean thought he heard Stan and Ollabell talking to him, but they denied it. "I believe it's coming from that puddle," Ollabell said. In fact, it was, for Sean and the pine heads had come to one of the crossroads along the path where the little black eyes were waiting for a stranger to pass.

However, these mischievous creatures had never met a clever rabbit before, and Sean was not easily tricked. Only with an extraordinary effort were these pesky critters able to misdirect him as he searched for Violet and the river.

Soon Sean found himself in the part of the woods where sleeping without a fur coat could be dangerous. The next morning, he and the pine heads awoke covered in frost, as if they had been sugared. This was the labor of the tiniest inhabitants in the woods; about the size of ants, the frosty creatures were called frost fairies. Looking under leaves and on grass, you might think them to be jewels, but they were really living creatures that blew shimmering white frost over everything—people, animals, the green leaves, moss, grass, clover, and the rocks of the river—just before dawn. When they did, they made the most enchanting sounds, like tiny crystal bells ringing; a sound practically undetectable to the insensitive ear.

Avoiding the grass goblins' bites and pinches, wasting valuable time with wrong directions from the deceiving little black eyes, and thawing out from the work of the frost fairies—all the while listening to the pine heads talking, eating, and arguing—fully occupied Sean's days and nights. Ollabell and Stan even began to nag him to leave this land with no river or river goddess, as it seemed. It was all beginning to get on his nerves and dampen his spirits. His great adventure felt as though it might have been a bad idea, a silly prospect, and that maybe he had made a promise he couldn't keep. *Perhaps, after all, I really am just a shiftless, worthless, conniving, big-mouthed thief!* he thought, feeling very, very sorry for himself. But worst of all, Sean began to wonder if he were just a dreamer of a ridiculous plan.

Chapter Five

Tears for a River

That night, the moon was a swollen ball of white light in a clear black sky as a thick fog of sadness enveloped Sean. He wandered haphazardly into a small clearing in the middle of nowhere, while Ollabell and Stan slept soundly in the sack that was strung across his shoulders and hanging down his back.

Lingering in the air, the scent of pine welcomed him, and he noticed a small blue spruce tree standing alone in the center of the clearing. Exhausted and despondent, Sean sat down near the tree, as if it were a comforting stranger. It wasn't too long before he was overcome by a powerful urge to unburden his soul.

"My name is Sean," he said to the tree. "I come from a troubled forest, an old wood with no river, where everyone is dying. I thought I could bring the water back if I found the river goddess. I've really never done anything good for anyone. I'm just a thief." Tears ran down his face. He looked at the little quiet tree.

"But there is one thing that matters to me more than anything: I love Meeka; I always have, from the first time I saw her. I want to bring the river to the troubled forest for her. I believed I could, but now I just don't know." Sean started crying again. "I don't care if I am lost forever; I probably am anyway, so who cares!"

Awakened by Sean's tormented words, Ollabell and Stan climbed out of the bag, wrapped their long, skinny arms around his neck, and cried too.

From the shadow of the tree came the sound of a jingle. Sean saw that it came from Robert Snow, who stepped out from under the tree accompanied by the tiniest turtle Sean had ever seen. *Turtles like rivers,* Sean thought.

His eyes swollen and red and his nose running, Sean asked the rat if he were the river goddess in disguise.

The rat shook his head "no"; he took a tiny handkerchief from his pocket and handed it to the sniffling rabbit.

"Oh," sighed Sean sadly, blowing his nose and wiping it. "Then do you know where I can find her?"

Just then, Sean felt a nudge on his back.

"Stop it, Ollabell!" he said impatiently. "Not now."

"It's not me, Sean," she replied, from his shoulder.

"It's not me, either," said Stan, from the other shoulder.

All of a sudden, Sean heard the most beautiful sound he had ever experienced: bubbling, rolling, soothing, liquid sounds of water running over thick moss-covered rocks.

He whirled around to behold a deer, just inches from him, as it nudged him again with its nose. Sean held his breath. *Deer are naturally timid creatures; don't move, Sean, don't move,* he reminded himself. Sean didn't want it to run away, and his mind raced ahead with the thought, *This must be her!*

This must be her! He couldn't move. *Should I say something?* he pondered.

For once, Ollabell was speechless, as she and Stan stood frozen on the rabbit's shoulders.

The sound of running water became even louder now, and the forest around them suddenly seemed full of life. You could just feel it. Moving only his eyes, Sean looked around from side to side. He was awed by what he saw in the light of the moon and millions of stars: a shimmering flowing river several yards to the side of the deer. The thick lime-green moss that covered the river rocks glowed like the moss in the tunnel, making the rocks sticking up from the water and on the sides look like giant emerald jewels.

The tree trunks were covered, too, as if they were wearing green wooly coats. And under Sean's furry paws, the ground was soft and moist. In the distance, he saw the outline of a tall mountain settled under a violet-blue night sky, and he heard the unmistakable sound of a waterfall nearby. The air was noticeably cooler and fresher, and incredible scents of wild thyme, rosemary, lavender, pine, sweet lilies, and wild spicy petunias filled the night air as if it were the river's perfume.

Ollabell sucked in a deep breath. "Mmm, doesn't that smell delicious? Stan, have you ever smelled such—"

"Shhhhh," said Sean, expecting the deer to take off. Instead, it calmly turned, walked to the edge of the river, and drank from it.

"She really is here!" Sean whispered to Robert Snow, almost in disbelief. "That's Violet, right?"

Robert Snow just smiled, as if confirming that the deer was the river goddess.

Then, from somewhere behind the pine tree on the edge of the clearing, came the whistling sound of an arrow. Someone was shooting at them! Startled, the graceful creature leaped into the river. Sean looked around. He could just make out the haunted, decrepit figure of a hunter, dead but not dead—the ghost of Angus Gunne. The ghost was screaming at Sean, "No! I will kill you, too! She's mine. Get away! I've waited all these years, and now you've brought her to me. Argh! I should thank you, but I won't." Another arrow flew by them as the ghost hunter charged at the group like a wild maniac.

This was the part of the story that Carol couldn't bring herself to tell the animals that night in the forest when she had read to them just after Sean left. As the rest of the story goes:

Soon after Daniel left the Kingdom of Teru, his father, King Moran, sent out fifty of his best trackers and expert hunters to bring him back. The king refused to let his only son go off to become an explorer and insisted that Daniel would be king someday, because the king's daughter, Lydia Rose—whom he said was far too gentle and silly and refused to hunt—could never be a good queen. Even though the people loved her dearly, he could not allow that to happen.

Angus Gunne was the best tracker of all the fifty, as well as the most skilled hunter, and it was he who found Daniel in Violet's woods. That was, indeed, a difficult thing to do, since few had ever found the woods and even fewer ever left it—a fate he would share. Carefully concealing himself, Angus spent weeks observing Daniel and the deer. By day, they would quietly stay by the river or walk through the forest, and they remained inseparable even at night, he observed. It was clear to him that they were in love.

The river goddess's beauty captivated Angus, and he desired her more and more each night, especially when he saw her transform from the deer into Violet. He convinced himself she would be his, not Daniel's, but that was impossible, because the bond between Daniel and Violet was unbreakable and not simply a mortal love.

The tracker grew more jealous, more envious, every day, and it choked any virtue he had ever had out of him. His mind became twisted and poisoned. His schemes to separate the pair and have Violet for himself varied from taking Daniel back to Teru—where he would be forced to be king or imprisoned by his own father—to just plain killing him now. One evening just before sunset, as the deer was about to enter the water to become Violet, the crazed hunter placed an arrow in his bow, pointed it at Daniel, and released it. Seeing Angus fire, the deer ran toward Daniel to block the arrow with her own body, but it was too late. The arrow struck Daniel in the back, and he fell to the ground.

Daniel struggled to his feet, turned, and saw the man. "Quick, Violet, run!" he gasped, as he fell into the river, bleeding badly.

Violet, who had thought him invincible and forgotten that he was just a mortal man, watched as he died right there in front of her . . . calling her name before disappearing under the water.

Before the jealous murderer could shoot again, Violet, who was still in the form of a deer, leaped into the air and knocked the hunter to the ground with a swift blow to his head, killing him. Then she jumped into the river after Daniel, and they were never seen together again. With the disappearance of Daniel and Violet, the river just vanished, evaporating into the sky, or so it seemed.

But Sean had thought differently when he had read the story, for he knew that a love like that doesn't simply disappear. He had believed the river goddess and the river still existed, and now here she was and so was the river. What he could not have known was that the ghost of the tracker Angus Gunne still haunted the woods, and Angus's hate and jealousy and need for revenge allowed him to retain solid form in this enchanted forest.

Another arrow flew by Sean . . . then another . . . and another. Only the quickness and skill of Sean's rabbit feet saved him from being hit and killed. Stan and Ollabell let go of Sean's neck and tumbled to the ground, scurrying under the pine tree along with Robert Snow and the little turtle.

Having emptied his quiver by now, Angus fumbled around on the ground searching for more arrows. Sean looked at the river for the deer. He heard another whistling sound. Whirling around, with the super-speed hands of a master magician—or, in his case, thief—Sean caught an arrow aimed at his heart. Having no more ammunition, Angus pulled out a long sword and came at Sean. They both tumbled into the river, causing Angus to drop his sword, which swiftly sank to the bottom. Sean struggled under the water, kicking as hard as he could, but Angus was much bigger and stronger and managed to hold Sean down with one hand as he struggled to reach his sword with the other.

Recovering their courage, Ollabell and Stan ran to the river's edge carrying armfuls of the small pinecones that had fallen to the ground beneath the pine tree they were hiding under. With all their puny might, they threw them one after the other at Angus, but still he held the rabbit under the water. Close on the heels of the pine heads, emboldened by their action, Robert Snow ran up to them yelling as loudly as a rat could, "If only Sean could call her name. Why don't you try?"

"Oh, yes! We could try!" Ollabell shouted back to him.

Ollabell yelled, "Violet! Help the rabbit!" Then Stan and Ollabell called out together, "Violet! Violet! Violet! Please! Help our friend, Sean!" No one had called out Violet's name for a very long time. Not since Daniel's death.

Angus found the sword, clutched its handle under the water, and drew it up into the sky to strike a mortal blow to the drowning rabbit.

A forceful gust of wind blew. As if time had sped up, the moon disappeared quickly from sight behind fast-swirling clouds. The river water churned unusually, and the current came to a sudden halt. Lightning flashed, and thunder rumbled in the sky. With a mighty crackle, a lightening bolt struck the river, forcing Angus away from Sean. The powerful blow knocked the sword out of Angus's hand and back into the water, where it sank to the bottom once again. Stan, Ollabell, and Robert fell to the ground, too. The rabbit lay at the bottom of the river, next to the fallen sword. Before them, a swirl of water like a funnel rose from the surface and then fell. And there, where the swirl had been, was Violet, the river goddess, towering over them all.

Just as the book had described her, she had long, dark hair like the black soil of the river bottom and deep green eyes the color of the lush moss that covered the rocks and tree trunks. Her dress flowed like watery soft fabrics of green and blue silks and velvet. She reached under the water, scooped up the rabbit in one hand, and brought him to her.

The ghost tracker, without his deadly arrows or sword, realized that he was no match for a river goddess and fled into the dark of night.

The clouds parted and moonlight fell upon the soaked, limp body of Sean, now cradled gently in Violet's folded arms. She examined his ear. She spoke softly but commandingly to the pine heads. "This rabbit is not from these woods, yet he wears the symbol of the Great Watcher. Why is this?"

Trembling, the pine heads stood up, as Ollabell haltingly questioned Violet, "Sean . . . Sean . . . he's not dead, is he?"

"Ah, so you care for this rabbit, do you?" Violet replied.

"Oh, yes, yes, we do! Don't we, Stan?"

"Oh, yes, we do!" exclaimed Stan.

"He is a very brave rabbit, even if he is a thief and a little crazy. He promised to bring this river back to his forest. He wants to race you for it," Ollabell added.

"Ollabell, you shouldn't say so much!" scolded Stan.

"Race me for the river?" Violet repeated, with a gentle laugh.

"Yes, yes, for the forest . . . but mostly for love; he loves someone named Meeka and wants to do it for her," added Ollabell, ignoring Stan's admonition.

"Ollabell, now you *have* said too much!" Stan demanded.

"Hush, pine heads!" commanded Violet, who wanted to know more about this strange creature. "For love, you say? This little creature?" she added, staring at the piteous body of Sean in her arms. "I use to care for . . . I loved . . . someone . . . long ago," she mused. "But how does a common rabbit thief know of such love?"

The rat stepped forward, offering, "Perhaps you should ask him; he has come far and risked much for this promise."

"Such a wise rat," agreed Violet, and she held the rabbit's body up to the sky.

"Awake, noble rabbit, from your watery sleep! Awake, hero thief, and tell the secrets you keep!"

Violet spoke these words over and over again until, finally, Sean sputtered out water and moved. His eyes fluttered open, and he realized that he was in the arms of the river goddess. Her beauty was beyond any idea he'd had of her. He gazed around silently and spotted Ollabell, Stan, and Robert standing forlornly on the riverbank.

Violet broke his spell with, "So, I understand that you wish to race me for the river, noble rabbit hero thief?"

"Yes . . . yes . . . I do," came Sean's weak, but still determined, response.

"And why is that?" Violet asked, already knowing much of the reason.

"Because the forest has no water. Because the animals are dying."

"But you're a thief. What do you care?"

"I care! And I said I would do it. I am a very fast runner. The fastest in the forest!"

"Yes, so I've heard, but I've also heard more; such as you are doing this for love."

Sean didn't know how to answer her. He was feeling too shy to talk of such things with a river goddess—or anyone, really. Telling the little pine tree was the first time he'd ever spoken about this.

"Who is Meeka?" Violet asked him.

"A wild horse," Sean answered.

"A wild horse and a rabbit?" said Ollabell.

"Yes, I know, but I love her like you loved Daniel," Sean said to the goddess.

There was an uncomfortable silence for a few moments until Violet spoke again: "Yes, I loved once," she admitted, as a tear ran down her cheek and fell into the river, the first time such a thing had ever happened to her. "I still do; for you see, little one, we both share this uncommon love you speak of. Nevertheless, love is love." More tears fell down her cheeks and into the water. The river seemed to be rising and moving faster.

Regaining her composure, Violet said, "Tell me, Sean, does she love you back?"

"I don't know. I've never told her how I feel, and I don't think I ever will."

"Ah, unexpressed love; what a waste! Such a bold creature, such as yourself, why do you fear to tell her? Words of love are as powerful as a river. Did you know that, rabbit?"

Sean listened. He thought he understood. "Okay, I will tell her when I bring the river to the forest. I will tell her it is for her! I love her, and I promised I would bring *her* the river."

Then Sean became very quiet, adding, "If she is still alive, that is; she was very weak and wounded when I left."

"Now I see why the Great Watcher gave you his symbol," Violet said. "You are much more than meets the eye. Well, then, I will grant you your wish: I'll race you for the river. But I must warn you about such a challenge, because the river is really not mine to give or take. I cannot guarantee the outcome even if you, by some miracle, should win. And if you lose . . . well, the consequences to you could be . . . well, I just cannot know."

"I accept!" Sean hastily replied, perhaps too weakened by his near-death experience to fully realize what he was doing.

A wall of water was building behind Violet as she placed Sean on the riverbank next to the pine heads and Robert Snow. Sean looked at the three of them—his faithful comrades, his friends in this great adventure—quizzically . . . pleadingly . . . not knowing how to say what he so wanted to ask of them.

"Come on, we're going with him!" exclaimed Ollabell, not waiting for the unneeded answer from Stan as the pine heads climbed together into the sack.

"I'm coming too," said Robert, "if you'll have me. A poet cannot avoid such an honorable adventure as this, for love, the greatest of all reasons."

The rat ran up Sean's leg, the bell jingling, and he climbed into the sack with Stan and Ollabell. All three heads popped out of the top of the sack to watch what would happen next.

As the water moved toward them, Violet melted silently into the river, leaving Sean newly restored and energized by the faith of his friends and the adventure ahead. He took off "like a rabbit" and headed for the woods. Without fanfare, the race was on! He knew that he must get to the tunnel entrance just before the river; it was time to put his plan into action.

Grass goblins grabbed at him from the lumps of grass, and little black eyes called to him as he leaped over puddles. He tore through the thick forest, and the green world in the moonlight was a blur to him.

In the light of the oncoming dawn, Sean saw what he was looking for. Still standing upright at the vine-covered rock wall next to the tunnel entrance was the hollowed-out tree trunk he had put there for just this moment. He pulled it to the ground and leaped in just as the wall of water crested. The small boat floated up onto the rushing wave as it roared into the darkness of the tunnel passage.

Where is Violet, he wondered? Was he now just racing the river? Had Violet stayed in her woods? Maybe he had already won, and she had given him the river. Or maybe this was just a dangerous trick. *After all,* he thought, *how could any mere mortal know what a river goddess would—could—do?* True, she had saved his life, but still, it was impossible to know what would happen next.

Around miles and miles of curves and turns, like a great rollercoaster, the rabbit, the rat, and the two pine heads rode in the tree-trunk boat.

Blasting out from the opening in the stone wall, the water burst into the daylight. The snow was gone; the valley was green. The water carried the craft past the haunted forest of giants and past the mountain where the Great Watcher had given Sean his tattoo. All was quiet; no sign of any sheep or the Great Watcher himself. The river swiftly flowed past the pine trees where Stan and Ollabell were from. Even if they had wanted to get out, it was too late. The river seemed to be going even faster now, as if it had a mission and a destination of its own.

Sean would have to be ready for the next phase of his plan: when they were almost to the field where Mercury had been taken, he planned to jump from the boat. He may have been thought of as just a stupid rabbit thief, but Sean had a clever and inquisitive mind. Among the many bits of useful information he had picked up in his life was the knowledge that the shortest distance between two points is a straight line. Knowing that the old river channel followed a winding path through the field and into the forest, he knew that he could get ahead of it if he were on foot following a direct path through landscape he knew like the back of his own paw. His plan depended upon being able to get in front of the river as it entered the forest so that it would follow him.

It was almost time to jump ship, for he saw the field in the distance. "Hang on tight!" Sean yelled out to the three terrified creatures in his sack.

"Sean, look out!" warned Stan.

Sean turned to see a massive buffalo made of water only a few feet behind him. The river water was furiously fast. In the distance, Sean could make out the outline of the troubled forest. The race was going to be even closer than he had imagined.

"You can do it, Sean! Your courage is your great fortune!" screamed Robert Snow, with as much authority as he could muster above the roaring river noise and his own sense of terror.

"Hold on!" shouted Sean, as he leaped from the hollowed log and hit the ground running, his huge hind legs churning like windmill blades.

As he ran past the field at blinding speed, a hunter caught sight of him and released his molf on the rabbit. At the front of the field, harnessed to a heavy wooden cart piled with bodies of slaughtered animals and metal traps, was Mercury. He saw the rabbit running ahead of the wall-of-water buffalo, with the dreaded molf and hunter in hot pursuit, at an angle that would bring them across his path. As the molf was about to pass in front of him, Mercury reared into the air in a mighty fury, breaking his harness apart. The tight straps holding him fell to the ground, and his powerful front legs rose high in the air, pawed briefly at the sky, and came murderously down on the unsuspecting molf.

The hunter, running breathlessly behind, had his bow and arrow and all of his concentration aimed at the rabbit, and, like his molf, failed to see the fate awaiting him. Once again, Mercury reared up, hooves poised, and came down like a thunderous lightning bolt. Sean would continue on his journey without fear from these two fiends ever again.

"The rabbit is coming! Sean's coming! And he has the river!" called Jimmy the squirrel from the treetops. All the animals except Meeka and Finn hurried to the edge of the forest. The bear hadn't left Meeka's side since the night Sean had departed. With so little water and food, not to mention her broken heart and battered body, Meeka was weak and barely clinging to life. There wasn't much Finn could do for her with just his herbs and roots.

"Make a path for him! Here he comes, the rabbit thief, with the river! I can't believe it! I can't believe it!" shouted Edward, startled, and tremendously excited—perhaps for the first time in his life.

Finn whispered to Meeka, hoping she could hear him. "Sean has come back, Meeka, and he has brought the river with him. Hold on, dear one."

Sean flew past them, with the water buffalo breathlessly close behind. If it caught him, Sean knew that he would lose the river—and probably his life as well. Through the forest he knew so well, he led the water creature on a tortuous new river channel that curved around trees and big rocks toward his destination on the far side.

And it was there, at the steep and high cliffs, where Sean leaped to the edge, daring the river and buffalo to tumble over. If Sean could create a waterfall here, the river would never again be lost to the forest; it would have to stay with the animals forever. He would be a hero, and he wouldn't have to steal anything ever again! (Well, maybe not as much, anyway.)

But just then, the creature came to an earth-wrenching, screeching stop. And, of course, the rest of the roaring river had to stop behind it. "Come on, come on," Sean teased. "The race is not done. Otherwise, I win, and the river is here to stay. Come on, you stupid ugly coward!" he yelled at the buffalo, taunting him. But to no avail, for the beast merely snorted a ton of water in Sean's direction and stood its ground.

I must do something to provoke him, the rabbit thought. Sean yawned, mocking the buffalo, as if it were no challenge at all for him. "Ah, you watery fool, you are no match for me. See, I am already bored with you and this silly race." Sean yawned again.

The buffalo angrily snorted another barrel or so of water toward Sean. "It was so easy to win!" said the now-drenched rabbit, feigning another huge yawn. Secretly, to himself, he heaved an inward sigh of relief, for he was absolutely exhausted, and, truth to tell, he wasn't so sure that he could have run much farther.

By this time, most of the animals in the forest had caught up to the action at the cliffs to watch the showdown and were cheering Sean on. Most, that is, except for Grandpa Raccoon; he had died just a few nights before. But as Grandma Raccoon, riding atop a giant frog as if he were her wheelchair, passed by Finn and Meeka, she told them that Sean had made it to the cliffs.

"Do you hear that, Meeka? Sean is already at the cliffs. Can you hear them cheering for Sean and the river?" Finn asked.

Meeka lay there weak and silent but then mustered the strength to lift her head ever so slightly and whisper, "Yes, I think I can hear them. Please, Finn, help me up; I must be there to see this."

The forest animals looked on in terrified awe as Sean continued his dangerous antics with the buffalo, trying desperately to provoke the beast into getting close enough to the cliff edge that it might fall over, taking the river along. It moved nearer to him, then nearer. It scraped the ground with its watery hooves. A gust of wind blew hard, and the leaves on the trees pressed back. At that moment, a swirl of water, like a funnel, arose from the river and settled down over the buffalo to reveal Violet astride the creature as it continued its cautious advance toward Sean.

"Stop!" she ordered the buffalo.

"I have won. The river is here!" Sean called out jubilantly.

"No, Sean. I told you that the river is not something that can be won or possessed," Violet corrected him, as the river started to recede, retracing its course away from the cliff.

"No!" Sean screamed, as he leaped onto the buffalo in front of Violet.

Before Violet could stop him, Sean dug his muscular hind feet into the buffalo's sides as hard as he could, causing the creature to lurch forward and carry them toward the cliff's edge.

"Catch!" Sean called out to the crowd, tossing his sack full of Stan, Ollabell, and Robert Snow. Edward caught the bag with his good wing and tumbled the contents out onto the ground. All three passengers were disoriented from the rollercoaster ride but managed to wobble over to join the rest of the group watching the action unfold.

"Stop, you crazy rabbit. Stop! You'll destroy yourself. Stop!" Violet called out.

"Oh, Sean, please stay with us," yelled Ollabell. "The river is here now!"

"You did it, Sean! You brought them the river, my dear friend," cried out Stan.

"Sean, you're the greatest hero I have ever known. It was a great honor to know and travel with you," shouted Robert Snow, wiping the tears from his face with the same tiny handkerchief that he had lent Sean.

Now all of the forest animals were screaming at Sean, begging him to rein in the creature he was forcing to carry him into oblivion. Their shouts and tears rained down upon his huge ears, almost drowning out the roar of the water itself.

But it was way too late. No power on earth, not even a river goddess, could prevent Sean and the river from sailing over the cliff at breakneck speed. The animals all scrambled to look down over the edge as the water crashed thunderously onto the boulders at the very bottom. They stared in shock and amazement as the river continued on down the valley past the boundaries of the troubled forest for miles and miles. Soon, there was nothing to see but an enormous pool at the bottom of the new waterfall—not a sign of Sean or Violet or the buffalo. Nothing but cool, clean, clear, life-sustaining water as far as the eye could see.

Mercury, having escaped the slavery of the hunters, had followed the river and managed to catch up to the crowd. Arriving just in time to see Sean ride the buffalo to a certain death, he was dumbstruck; then he spied Meeka with Finn. Certain that she had been killed when he was captured, he could barely contain his emotion as he galloped to the side of his beautiful mate.

Almost too weak to recognize him, Meeka allowed herself to be nuzzled by Mercury as she slowly regained her senses. Finn had collected water from the new river and brought it to her. He got her to take a sip, then another; this was not just ordinary river water, and its recuperative powers were felt almost immediately. Meeka opened her eyes and saw Mercury standing above her, and the joy of their reunion was itself a source of legendary stories repeated for many generations around the campfires of the forest.

And it wasn't too long before the few remaining hunters and their molfs left the area, for they were no longer able to take advantage of a troubled forest that was no longer troubled. With no sick and hungry animals to prey upon anymore, the evil predators fell upon hard times and began fighting among themselves, killing one another.

That spring, when the forest was blossoming as it hadn't for many years and was turning the most beautiful green anybody had ever seen, all the animals, including Meeka and Mercury's healthy new twin foals, Sean and Violet, held a ceremony to celebrate the miraculous restoration. Every single creature from the forest was there, including the newest inhabitants: Ollabell, Stan, and Robert Snow.

They all assembled by the clear, cool, pool of water at the bottom of the waterfall, and there, standing next to his dear friend Finn, was Edward, the newly elected Grand Vizier of the Great Forest. With tears welling in his eyes, Edward spoke these humble words: "We are gathered here today to honor the memory of Sean, our beloved rabbit thief, who stole our hearts and gave us back this river that sustains our lives. From

this day forward, it shall be known as the Yawning Rabbit River." With that, a giant golden carp leaped from the water and gracefully arced back into it with a huge, crowd-spraying splash.

As the thunderous applause died down, the animals of the Great Forest dried their tears, hugged each other tenderly, and went their separate ways home. Tranquility had returned to this idyllic place, and it would not be disturbed again for many generations.

OLD MILLER HOUSE

Part II
(Many Years Later)

The Big House

Chapter Six

New Things

The big house had been built on the very hill where Mercury and Meeka and their offspring had once run free and grazed upon the rich green grass and clover. But that was long ago—a forgotten time, except that in the distant outlying valleys, shepherds still spoke of wild horses.

The opulent mansion had dozens of large rooms, all with tall windows looking out onto the meticulously manicured hedges and plantings. Not a leaf was out of place on the perfectly cut lawns that instead were cluttered with more than twenty imported, ridiculous, marble statues sporadically placed throughout.

The owners, Harold and Harriet Miller, had moved to Briarwood from Port Olive, the busy coastal city on the Great Ocean, no doubt because land was so much less expensive here. As evidence, when Mrs. Miller took guests she wanted to impress on a tour of her big house and sprawling property, she would boast, "Oh, you get so much more for your money here. Look how big the house is and look how much land we have. Ha, ha, ha, ha, ha!" she would laugh excitedly, intoxicated by her self-proclaimed genius in purchasing it.

To fill the lofty rooms and long echoing hallways had required ten moving vans, traveling single file in a line over the steep and treacherous Laughing Wolf Pass, filled with all the Millers' "stuff." For example, there were the several thousand fancy leather-covered books that would never be read or appreciated. They were just for show, much like silent, well-behaved children, and used only to fill the decorative shelves of Mr. Miller's wood-paneled office—wood cut from the oldest oak trees in the surrounding forest.

Then there was Mrs. Miller's one-of-a-kind cruel umbrella collection: over one hundred of them, with ornately carved handles of elephant, hippopotamus, and walrus tusk; rhinoceros horn; monkey bone, tiger bone, and whalebone; and deer antler. At each of the twelve entrances to the mansion was an assortment of these hideous umbrellas, obsessively used to guarantee keeping the rain off Mrs. Miller's elaborate, sprayed hairdos. "Oh, there's that horrible rain again!" she would yell, as if it were somebody's fault.

There was actually a whole truck just for her appliances; she collected all kinds of ice-cream makers, popcorn poppers, donut-making machines, muffin bakers, cotton-candy machines, hot dog broilers, French fryers, automatic cookie cutters, electronic nut crackers, potato mashers, barbecued-chicken roasters, and so on, and so on. The truck also contained the dozens of radios and televisions that would always be left on in a room, insuring a constant noise to block out any evidence of a bird's song, the sound of "that horrible rain," or the call of the wind outdoors in nature. And amazingly, as if what they already owned weren't enough, Mr. and Mrs. Miller were often away buying even more things.

Now when Harriet Miller was home, she mostly spent her days in her big bed, leaning against her pink-dyed, rabbit-fur pillows and wearing her matching pink rabbit-fur slippers and, of course, lots of her favorite jewelry. The television was invariably tuned to her favorite game show or shopping channel. On the bed were plates of yummy snacks, as she called them, such as sugared donuts, hot dogs, French fries, candied popcorn, hot fudge ice-cream sundaes, sticky cinnamon muffins, or cotton candy. She would happily munch away on them while wiggling her toes, looking through mail-order catalogs and magazines, and checking off things to buy. All the while, her little white dog, Princess Cookie, hopped over her— back and forth, barking in a high-pitched squeak—as if Mrs. Miller were a great big log, which, in fact, she was well on her way to resembling.

As for her husband, the peculiar Harold Miller occupied himself all day—and most nights, being a bit of an insomniac—in his office, buying and selling all kinds of things by phone or mail. He had file cabinets filled to overflowing with notebooks, receipts, and lists of all kinds, showing purchases and sales. He went over them repeatedly and constantly walked around the house, notebook in hand, as he counted everything he had purchased . . . as if the things might have disappeared overnight.

One time, while on a buying trip, the Millers traveled by way of a luxury cruise ship across the Great Ocean, and it was on this trip that they brought home something very different from their typical purchases: twin baby boys. They had purchased the boys from one of the shady passengers, who was illegally smuggling the babies abroad in hopes of selling them for a big price in Port Olive. He had settled for much less when Mrs. Miller discovered the twins and made him an "offer he couldn't refuse," having threatened to tell the authorities what he was doing if he didn't accept it.

Harriet Miller seemed thrilled with the discounted babies—no doubt because they were such a bargain—and called them Ash and Dusty for no better reason than that she had been dusting off an ashtray while thinking about names. In her usual bad taste, when the Millers had guests, she would bring the babies into the parlor after dinner and exclaim, delightedly and loudly, "Pairs are always better in any purchase, right Mr. Miller? Ha, ha, ha, ha!"

Except for the fact that the twin brothers looked so much alike, both had dark hair and brown eyes, the two babies grew up to be very different boys. Dusty was shy, gentle, and soft spoken, while Ash was loud, boisterous, and prone to insulting or striking. People would say that there was something wrong with little Dusty, in an effort to explain why he was such a quiet child, all the while dismissing Ash's abominable behavior as just being that of a typically active boy.

When the twins played outside, Dusty would walk carefully in Briarwood Forest. From an early age, he had a gift for knowing birds, plants, and flowers and enjoyed collecting seeds and growing them. Ash, on the other hand, ran noisily through the woods, breaking branches, banging birds' nests out of the trees, and terrorizing the small animals. He'd trap squirrels, turtles, mice, snakes, groundhogs, rabbits, little birds—anything he could catch—and torment them by locking them up in closets or tying them up under the beds to scare his parents or the household help.

As a little boy, Dusty came to know Briarwood Forest well, sometimes spending the whole day there. He sat by the Yawning Rabbit River listening to the sound of the moving water running as if it were a language he understood. It seemed he preferred the music of the river to any other voice.

One spring afternoon, when the twins were about to turn nine years old, Dusty returned from the river and found a box sitting on the front porch. He was used to seeing sometimes up to fifty boxes being delivered in one week, so he paid it no attention until he heard some rustling coming from inside. Just then, the front door flew open, and Mrs. Miller, with Princess Cookie in her arms, called out, "Oh, good. Harold! Mr. Miller! The package is here. Ash! Dusty! This is for you."

Ash pounced through the doorway, ready to tear open the box. "I want it!" Ash yelled, starting to pull at the top.

"Careful now, Ashy; it's for you both. I bought two, you know. Pairs are always better!"

"What is it? Not dumb dogs, I hope. And I hate cats!" Ash snapped.

"No, no, no, it's much better than that. I saw them in the back of a magazine last month and on sale!" she boasted. "I got a very good deal."

Mr. Miller arrived at the door with his pencil and notebook in hand.

"Open it, open it, Mr. Miller!" she commanded, but Ash beat him to it and pulled open the top. They all looked into the open box except Dusty, who stood away from the frenzy.

"What's that?" said Ash, backing away.

"Oh, there's just one, and it's strange. That's not what I ordered!" blurted Mrs. Miller. "Mr. Miller, there's just one and—what *is* that?"

Princess Cookie yapped at whatever they were looking at in the box.

Dusty walked cautiously to the box and looked in. Sitting folded at the bottom, looking up, was a little boy with a gold coin for a head. He had large, expressive eyes and no mouth or nose.

"A coin-headed boy!" said Dusty, smiling down at him. He put out his hand to him.

"It's a freak!" Ash shouted into the box, "You're a freak!"

"Give me that receipt, Ash," Mr. Miller said, pointing to a piece of paper in the box.

"I'm not putting my hand in there with that thing!" spat back Ash.

"Yes, we must return it right away," said Mrs. Miller, peering over the box. "Ugh! See how it looks right into your eyes. Stop looking at me like that!" she yelled at the little boy. "It's so ugly," she added, wiggling her shoulders in a cold shiver of disgust. "Mr. Miller, do you think that its head is valuable? It looks like gold."

The coin-headed boy took the receipt from the box and handed it to Dusty. Obviously there was nothing wrong with his hearing or ability to understand.

Mrs. and Mr. Miller and Ash all jumped back.

Saying "Thanks," Dusty took the piece of paper and handed it to his father.

"It's from the Teru Toy Company," Mr. Miller read out loud, "and it's called a 'Penny Boy.' It doesn't say here what the head is made of, but . . . uh-oh," he muttered, pausing in mid-sentence, "it's stamped ABSOLUTELY NO RETURNS!"

"Oh, I didn't see that in the ad. I don't think it said that. No, that must be wrong! " declared Mrs. Miller. "Well, there's probably nothing we can do about it now anyway, and I really didn't pay much for it. Oh, just put it in the trash. We can't have that thing around here; I'm having a dinner party tonight for the senator and his wife. Dusty, first pull the coin off before you throw it away." Then she turned to go back into the house, holding tightly to Princess Cookie, who was still barking at the box.

"It's okay, Princess Cookie; it's okay, my precious," Mrs. Miller spoke soothingly to the yapping dog. Then, with a quick look at the sky, added, "Oh, no; it looks like rain. Ugh, that horrible rain!"

Mr. Miller scribbled something on the receipt, mumbled to himself about sales tax and shipping costs, and went back into the house to file the receipt. He figured that he'd check through his reference books for a Penny Boy toy to see if its head really was a valuable gold coin. Might yet be able to salvage something out of this mess his wife had made, he reasoned.

Dusty and Ash stood on the front porch by the box. "What are you lookin' at, you little freak!" yelled Ash. He took a pebble out of his pocket—from a stash he always carried for chucking at the poor creatures in the forest—and threw it at the boy's head. It made a metallic sound as it ricocheted off the big metal head. "Hah!" Ash laughed and ran down the steps. "Better get rid of that trash, Dusty!" he called back, heading down the long driveway.

"He's not trash!" Dusty shouted back at his brother, who was already out of earshot. Bending over the box, Dusty reached out toward the boy. "Come on out; they've all gone away." The little coin-headed boy grabbed Dusty's hand, stood up, took a fleeting look around, and stepped out of the box.

"Don't be frightened," said Dusty. "I'm not going to let them throw you away or take off your coin head. We'll figure out a way to keep you around until they get used to having you here . . . and that's a promise, 'Penny Boy.'" Dusty liked the name the toy company had given the boy, even if they hadn't really intended it as something personal. Besides, Dusty felt that this strange little person was somehow going to be very special and important in his life—something his brother, mother, and father had never been!

Chapter Seven

Something Old

Everywhere Dusty went, so did Penny Boy. After a while, Mr. and Mrs. Miller just sort of became used to seeing them together and stopped telling their son to "pull the coin off" or "throw him away in the trash."

"Penny Boy is the only one quieter than you, Dusty, but he doesn't have a mouth!" his mother would exclaim, then burst out laughing. Even Princess Cookie finally stopped yapping when she saw Penny Boy, and so, for a while, things seem to get better at the Miller house.

Dusty taught Penny Boy as much as he could, and when he discovered that his new friend could read, he began taking books from the house library for him. Dusty enjoyed sharing the history of Briarwood Forest and the Yawning Rabbit River with Penny Boy, who particularly loved sitting with Dusty atop Jumping Grace Waterfall at sunset, when the golden eagles would soar high above them and linger for a moment in the blue and orange sky.

When Dusty was twelve, he decided to build a greenhouse out of some wood and windows he found stored above the garage—scrap left over from the construction of the house. Penny Boy quickly became his enthusiastic helper. Dusty really loved growing flowers, and of all the photographs in the books that he and Penny Boy pored over, Dusty discovered that they shared the same favorite: roses. In his makeshift conservatory, Dusty was finally able to hybridize his very own variety of rose, a creation with a spectacular fragrance and gorgeous bright-yellow blossoms that were the same color as Penny Boy's own gold-coin head. Being a member of the Briarwood Rose Society (actually, the youngest ever; a real honor that puzzled his parents and enraged his brother), Dusty—in the tradition of rose growers throughout the world—registered the name in honor of his best friend: the Penny Boy. But Penny Boy was really more like Dusty's little brother.

Everyone who saw the extraordinary rose encouraged Dusty to enter it in competition. If he could win first prize, he'd have enough money to build a real greenhouse for his flowers, one with water and heat and lights. Not only that, but he could add a nice little room in it for Penny Boy, because Mrs. Miller wouldn't let him in the house. "He's too creepy!" she said, and made him sleep in the leaky, drafty, old tool shed near the garden. When they finished the makeshift greenhouse, Dusty helped Penny Boy move into that for the time being; no palace but better than the shed by far.

The following spring, around the time when Dusty would turn thirteen, he gave Penny Boy several gifts: pencils and paper to practice writing, a new blanket, a baseball, and a small metal box that held the special Penny Boy rose seeds. "You are in charge of these, Penny Boy," Dusty said solemnly, handing the box to him. Penny Boy held them close and vowed to himself to keep them hidden under his bed, safe from the prying eyes of Ash, who would have stolen them only to be vindictive because they were special to Dusty and Penny Boy.

As Ash grew older, his moods became darker and darker. One day, about three months before his and Dusty's thirteenth birthday, things got worse. Ash had followed the river farther than he had ever gone before, looking for frogs, snakes, and turtles to terrorize, when he caught sight of something shining in the clear water. It was an object wedged tightly between some river rocks just below the surface. He tugged on it until the riverbed finally loosened its grip, and he discovered that it was an old arrowhead. Amazingly, it was still so sharp that it had cut a deep gash into his right hand as he had pulled it out of the river. Ignoring the blood and pain, Ash wrapped his hand in the bright red bandanna he liked to wear around his neck, put the curious arrowhead in his shirt pocket, and trudged back home. That day, at least, the wildlife of the forest was safe from Ash.

Tragically, though, Ash was not safe from what he had awakened, for he had come across no ordinary artifact. This was the actual head from Angus Gunne's arrow: the very weapon that had pierced the heart of Daniel Moran and killed the river-goddess Violet's true love so long ago. It probably had been washed downriver in the race between Sean and Violet. Now Ash had somehow released the ghost of Daniel's murderer, the vengeful hunter Angus Gunne.

Ash's hand eventually healed—although he would always bear a scar—and his already-bad mood worsened day by day, night by night . . . as if he had become infected by hateful revenge. Ash fashioned a necklace out of the arrowhead and proudly wore the medallion over his chest for all the world to see, as if it were some kind of honor or award. Over the next few months, an eerie and strange permanent tattoo in the shape of the arrowhead appeared on the skin over Ash's heart. He was convinced that it meant something special and would give him extraordinary powers. He was horrifyingly right!

Chapter Eight

Broken Things

M r. and Mrs. Miller, with the yappy Princess Cookie in tow, were spending more and more time away from home on their buying trips, traveling the world to acquire even more "things" they really neither needed nor that made their lives any better for having.

Since they saw their children as just "acquisitions" anyway (which, in truth, they were), their care was left up to the household staff during these extended trips, so Dusty and Ash found themselves pretty much on their own. None of the housekeepers lived in; they just came during the day, did some cleaning and cooking, and then went home. They saw the boys before and after school for meals during the week, but evenings and weekends were more a matter of leftovers in the refrigerator and an almost total lack of supervision.

Dusty never had any illusions about the quality of his "parents" anyway, so not seeing them around the house for extended periods of time was more a relief than anything else. Penny Boy's care had been in his own hands ever since they'd unpacked him, so continuing to care for his friend presented neither hardship nor burden to the remarkable teenager. Ash, however, was another concern altogether, for he had always been "difficult" and now was totally unmanageable.

Most people, especially Mr. and Mrs. Miller, just found it easier to give in to Ash's temper tantrums rather than make any real attempt to guide the troubled boy into adulthood. For example, when Ash wanted a car, the Millers—never needing much of an excuse to buy something—just got him one, even though he was too young to have a driver's license by three years. Unfortunately for many of the animals that happened to cross the long driveway and the back roads, not to mention the occasional walker or biker, Ash's sadistic driving tendencies soon became legend in the neighborhood.

Shortly after the Millers had left on their latest buying trip, Ash began to talk in his sleep. Dusty slept in the bed across the room and was often awakened by his brother's disturbed conversations. Then, too, he became alarmed by the ghostly shadows that accompanied Ash's words, and it seemed that even the walls themselves hissed and snarled. It was around this time that a toxic black mold began to grow on the walls and ceilings of their bedroom, and no matter how well the cleaning staff scrubbed it off, the disgusting mold would return within a few days.

It was as if the house were haunted. Actually, the walls and ceilings were becoming infested with "soul crawlers," parasites of hate that thrived where evil lurked. Soon, the walls were alive with these hideous hidden creatures, man-eating worms that bit and could pull you into the walls if you got too close. The servants began to leave . . . or just plain disappear: first the gardener, then the cook, and then the full-time

"duster of things." It was as though they had all quit, which no sane person could blame them for doing, but they had left so many personal possessions behind—like coats and hats . . . even a purse—that it was impossible to know what had really happened. Of course, if the walls could have talked beyond the growls and moans they made, perhaps Dusty—now alone in the huge house with Ash—might have had even more reason to be concerned about his fate.

One night, in the dark of their bedroom, the crazy laughter and strange movements of Ash had, once more, awakened Dusty, who then lay awake watching the ghostly shadows move across the walls and ceiling. Hearing a fluttering sound of wings and a squeak of distress, he quickly jumped from the bed and turned on the lights. There, by Ash's bed, a robin was tethered to the lamp on the night table; a string tied to its wing was being pulled by Ash as he lay there. The poor bird's little wing hung limp and broken, its mouth wide open in sheer terror and pain.

Dusty raced across the room toward the robin, but Ash jumped up to block his way.

"What are you gonna do, fix its stupid wing? Some things are just too broken to fix . . . like you and Penny Boy . . . too stupid and broken ever since you were born!"

Ash had never before spoken in such poisonous and cruel tones to his brother, and Dusty's blood ran cold with the hatred he sensed was beneath those words.

"Move, Ash!" demanded Dusty and pushed on his brother's chest with both hands and all his might. "Owww!" he yelped, as his right hand caught on the arrowhead medallion underneath Ash's shirt, its sharp point cutting through the cloth and into his flesh.

Ash laughed in insane delight at his brother's pain.

Ignoring his stinging hand, Dusty began to untie the piteously fluttering bird. "Go away, Ash, just go away!" Dusty spat back at his brother. The coldness in his eyes left no doubt of the contempt he now felt toward Ash.

Dusty freed the bird and took it in his hands, heading for the greenhouse. Ash followed close behind, a shadowing figure that seemed much larger than he actually was.

Penny Boy peeked out from under his blanket as they entered the greenhouse and saw Dusty with the crippled bird. He felt a twinge of dread when he noticed Ash lurking behind.

As Dusty approached him, Penny Boy threw his covers back and jumped up from his cot, accidentally uncovering the metal box of rose seeds he always slept with.

"Aha!" exclaimed Ash. "What's that?"

Penny Boy looked down and saw that the box had been partially exposed. With a quick flick of the blanket, he covered it.

"Hiding something, you little loser?" Ash spat out, pulling the cover back.

"Those are just flower seeds, Ash. Penny Boy's in charge of them. They have nothing to do with you," said Dusty, who was calming the bird and stroking its head. Then, he gently handed the tortured creature to Penny Boy. "Hold it carefully; it's injured," he said. Then Dusty bent over and picked up the box just as his brother was reaching for it.

Ash watched this move with desperate eyes, looking at the metal box as if it were a hunted prey. His heart was more poisoned than ever. With a withering glance at both Dusty and Penny Boy, he ran out of the greenhouse without a word, like a wave suddenly and unnaturally receding into the ocean. *"I'll get my revenge,"* he mouthed silently in retreat.

Ash's abrupt departure made Dusty uneasy, but he was glad that his brother had left. There was no way to know just how dangerous Ash was becoming. Better to take care of the bird tonight; he'd try to deal with Ash tomorrow.

He put the metal box on the table and looked down at Penny Boy, who was comforting the bird. To Dusty's amazement, its injured wing was no longer broken. It was calm and appeared for all the world to have made a complete recovery.

"Penny Boy has magic hands," he said to the bird. Then he touched the boy's shoulder and marveled yet again at how his friend looked just as he had the day he'd arrived in the box: never aging, never growing. *Yes,* Dusty thought to himself, *there truly is something magical about Penny Boy.* "Great, Penny Boy; really wonderful."

Penny Boy stood up, cupping the bird gently in both his hands, and walked toward the door. Dusty took the metal box and followed him out into the night. The two stood there under the stars. "Okay, Penny Boy," signaled Dusty. Then Penny Boy opened his hands, and the bird flew away.

Dusty felt his hand throbbing and remembered the cut from Ash's arrowhead medallion. They returned to the greenhouse. Penny Boy took Dusty's hand and held it as he had the injured bird's wing; the wound stayed the same, but now the evil would never penetrate Dusty.

"Well, it is just a small cut," Dusty acknowledged, not realizing how Penny Boy's magic had just helped. "Thanks, though. I'll be fine."

They sat down together on the greenhouse floor, and Dusty, exhausted, fell fast asleep. Penny Boy held the metal box close to his chest, the precious treasure he had silently promised to protect. All around them in the greenhouse, rows of scented roses bloomed—an exhilarating sight on such a disturbing night.

In the early morning light, Dusty arose. Although better, his injured hand was still hurting and was a reminder of his encounter with Ash. He told Penny Boy that he'd be back in a little while, that he was going to see about Ash. But when he returned to the house, it appeared to be empty. In most of the rooms, the furniture had been overturned and broken apart. Shattered objects were everywhere. Although his car was parked in the driveway, Ash was nowhere to be found.

Long before daybreak, Ash, having wreaked havoc on the house in his fit of irritation over the bird—or the argument with his brother . . . or the metal box . . . or who knows what else—had disappeared into the woods. He had gone back to the place, down by the river, where he had found the arrowhead months ago. Picking up rocks, he began to throw them into the river, talking to himself and plotting in his mind how he would take the metal box from Penny Boy later.

With each strike of the water's surface by a rock, the river reacted with a splash. Bam! Another rock, then a big splash. The river water churned and rose in small peaks. Ash threw even harder, and the peaks became larger. He hurled yet another missile at an image in the water that looked to Ash like a dog's face made from ripples and swirls, but this time the huge rock never hit its target. A hand rose out of the water face and, with athletic reflexes, caught the rock in midair. Then the arm attached to the hand slowly emerged: it was the arm of an ancient water elemental, protector of the waters they live in.

It was an enormous, muscular arm that rose straight up into the air, and it was followed by the rest of a massive body

topped by the dog-like face of a pit bull with long black hair and a beard. Towering over the boy, the great form scooped up Ash as if he were a string bean ready to be eaten and held him suspended high in the air. Drawing Ash closer to its face, the elemental looked at the boy with its supernatural yellow eyes.

"You have disturbed the tranquility of the river," it bellowed at Ash, almost bursting the boy's eardrums. With that, it lowered the boy beneath the water's surface and held him there. Ash struggled to free himself, but it was pointless against the power of such a forceful being. When Ash had no more breath left, he felt the creature lift him out of the water. As soon as he emerged, Ash sucked in a great gulp of air and kicked hard at his captor.

The water elemental dropped Ash, who hit the water's surface hard and plunged down, down, down . . . as if there were no bottom to the river at all. It was more like an ocean this time. Before him, strange shadows and images passed through the watery realm. Ash struggled to know which way was up, and it was only the air from his own departing last breath that saved him. As the bubbles rose, he followed them to the surface and broke through. Gasping for air, he climbed onto the riverbank just as it began to rain. Thunder rolled across the sky, shaking the land. The water elemental had disappeared. Ash lay on the ground, altered and immobile: a usual state when having encountered a powerful phenomenon such as the water elemental.

Cold and angry, Ash returned to the house, all the while cursing the water creature, Dusty, and Penny Boy. "You'll all pay for this!" he muttered into the wind, over and over again.

It was later, under the cover of night, when Ash went to the greenhouse to seek the revenge he had promised his brother and Penny Boy. Peering in unobserved, he saw Dusty tending to his flowers as Penny Boy watched, holding the metal box under his blanket. Hidden from view except when the lightning lit the sky and property, Ash sat low to the ground under one of Mrs. Miller's monkey bone–handled umbrellas. He cursed the rain, as if the falling water were another one of his enemies. Nothing could wash away the darkness of his mood and the rage welling up within him.

Ash gripped the arrowhead medallion hanging around his neck tightly in his hand, not seeming to care that it was cutting into his skin. The blood ran down his arm and dripped off his elbow into a puddle of rainwater in front of him. With the next flash of lightning, Ash looked down and saw his reflection in the puddle of water and blood. He saw a face, but it was barely recognizable as his own; it was grotesquely distorted—like a picture of himself from a grim future, or a face from the past, like Angus Gunne, the hunter who had killed Daniel.

Ash decided that he would wait for Dusty and Penny Boy to fall asleep. He wanted the metal box of seeds. It represented something special: years of dedication to a hobby his brother loved. Ash had never known such a thing, something so simple. He hated the roses. He hated Penny Boy. *How could Dusty love such an ugly little freak?* he wondered. He was so far gone by this time that he hated his brother above all. Any chance of decency had flown away with the robin he had tormented the night before.

Throughout the night, inside the greenhouse, Dusty kept reassuring Penny Boy with, "Rest, Penny Boy; I'll look out for us."

His friend closed his worried eyes and drifted off to sleep, all the while clutching the seed box. Dusty watched him while he tended to the flowers and wondered if the little coin-headed boy ever had dreams. If he did, Dusty hoped they were peaceful ones.

Morning's first light streamed through the glass roof, turning the perfectly cared-for roses into an explosion of color so beautiful it could take your breath away. Dusty had finally given way to exhaustion and fallen asleep hunched over his beloved flowers. Penny Boy lay dozing on his cot, the box of precious seeds still in his arms.

Outside the greenhouse, the monkey bone–handled umbrella lay in the bloody puddle, but Ash was nowhere to be seen. Apparently, revenge against his brother and Penny Boy would wait for another day.

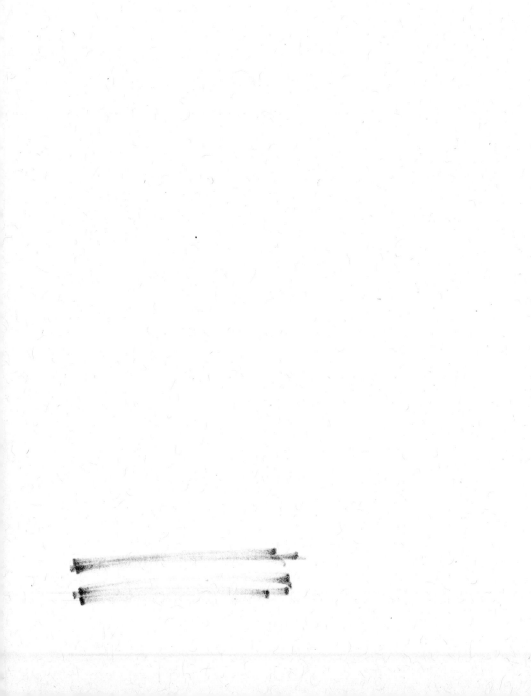

Chapter Nine

Into the Woods and Other Places

Dusty gently nudged Penny Boy awake. Penny Boy followed Dusty into the kitchen, where Dusty made himself some breakfast. He fixed nothing for Penny Boy because, very soon after his arrival, it became obvious to the Miller family that this strange little boy had no need for food, which was indeed fortunate since he had no mouth. They had all speculated upon this phenomenon but could reach no conclusion. Mrs. Miller was, of course, delighted, for she would have begrudged even giving Penny Boy table scraps. Dusty, with his special curiosity, marveled at the science of it all—being able to survive without obvious sustenance. Dusty finally decided that it was either a miracle or Penny Boy only needed light and air, like *Tillandsias*, those exotic air plants that grow and flourish without soil.

"We'll go down to the river this morning," Dusty told Penny Boy, who nodded his head in agreement. "Maybe we can find Ash there."

At the river, Dusty, exhausted from staying up almost all night guarding Penny Boy and the box, collapsed in the warmth of the sunlight by the river's edge. Penny Boy put the metal box he was carrying down by Dusty and began to play in the clear shallow water. He liked collecting different rocks and making tall piles of them, pretending they were buildings like those he saw in books about big cities—just like any regular child would do.

As Penny Boy played, a bird sang from the branch above. It flew down and hopped back and forth along the mossy river rocks near him. It was the very robin that he and Dusty had saved from Ash. Penny Boy sat on the grassy river edge and watched the bird. Suddenly, it flew from the rock, perched on top of his coin head and began dropping little flower seeds onto his lap. Penny Boy playfully pretended to eat them, even though he had no mouth. Out of his pocket, Penny Boy took a little toy he had found in the Miller's trash and always carried with him: a tiny silver bell on a purple ribbon. He put his finger in the air and the robin hopped onto it, whereupon Penny Boy brought the little bird to his lap and tied the bell around its head like a necklace.

Dusty woke to see his friend playing contentedly with the bird and stood up. Penny Boy knew that it was time to go back to the big house, for often each just seemed to understand what the other was thinking.

While walking back through the woods, Penny Boy watched the robin flying from branch to branch high above them all the way. *Just like a lookout*, he thought. Had the bird had the abil-

ity of speech, no doubt it would have warned them of what danger lay ahead.

Dusty saw Ash's car still parked in the same place in the driveway. The front door of the house was wide open, and they entered, Penny Boy still holding the metal box. Dusty called out for his brother, but there was no response.

They walked back out and around to the side of the house, and Dusty saw Ash run from the greenhouse. Dusty called out to him, but Ash ignored his brother. Penny Boy followed Dusty into the greenhouse, and Dusty gasped at the sight of the destruction. Every rose blossom had been cut off and tossed onto the ground—hundreds of them. The pots were overturned and broken, and the plants had been ripped apart, their roots destroyed. Years of Dusty's work lay in ruins on the ground.

"I want that box!" screamed Ash, lunging at Dusty through the open doorway.

Penny Boy, holding the container with the precious seeds tightly to his chest, ran out the door without Ash seeing him and hid behind the greenhouse wall. To Penny Boy, these were magic flower seeds; magic because Dusty had created them, and Penny Boy loved Dusty. He couldn't let this monster take them.

Ash knocked Dusty to the ground with a blow to the face, then began frantically searching for the metal box. "The little freak has them, doesn't he?" he roared. "Where are you?" Ash demanded, continuing his search for Penny Boy outside the greenhouse.

Ash went around the corner and saw the crouching boy. "Come back here!" he bellowed at the sight of the terrified Penny Boy, who had started running into the woods. "I'll kill that thing!" Ash yelled.

Dusty had regained consciousness and heard his brother yelling at Penny Boy. "Don't hurt him, Ash! They are only seeds! Stop this! I'll give them to you."

Ash ran into the woods after the boy but stopped in his tracks as he neared the river, then backed away. He quickly returned to the yard, got into his car, and raced down the long driveway. Turning onto a dirt path just barely wide enough for the automobile, he roared into the woods.

He drove crazily, turning down different paths, breaking branches, and crashing into bushes and small tress—all the while shouting out threats through the open windows: "I'll find you, freak. I'll find you and tear your head off . . . or whatever that thing is!" He was possessed. He drove in no particular direction and paid no attention. He just drove.

Dusty knew where Penny Boy might be and rushed to get there before his insane brother could find him. Dusty could hear the waterfall in the distance and hoped the boy would be there by the hollowed-out log. Sure enough, he found Penny Boy sitting on the log . . . and next to him was the robin, wearing its tiny bell on the purple ribbon.

Dusty was overjoyed to find Penny Boy safe; the seed box was resting on top of a tree stump nearby. Dusty gave Penny Boy a big hug and felt something under the boy's shirt.

"What's this?" Dusty asked, as Penny Boy handed him a cloth-covered object.

Dusty unwrapped it gingerly and found a faded green-covered book. "Where'd you find this, Penny Boy? It looks really old."

The boy pointed to the hollow of the log.

"Hmm, that log would be a good hiding place for the metal box if we need it, don't you think?"

Penny Boy nodded.

Dusty handed Penny Boy the book. "I'll come back for it later. Right now, I'd better look for Ash before he wrecks the car and kills himself . . . or somebody else. You stay here for now, and I'll come back for you, too. It's safer here than at the house, okay?"

Penny Boy took a scrap of paper and a pencil from his pocket and scribbled *I wait for Dusty*. It was the first time anyone had ever seen any of his writing.

"That's wonderful! Yes, you wait for me here."

Penny Boy sat on the log and picked up the metal box. He would protect it with his life if he had to.

Dusty left in a hurry to look for his crazed and troubled brother; he ran back to the house to see if Ash had returned. The car was nowhere in sight, but he found fresh tire tracks where the dirt road turned into the woods. Dusty had followed the tracks for about a mile when he saw it—the car was partially submerged in a swampy section of the river. Fearing the worst, Dusty rushed around to the driver's side to look inside. The car was empty. From behind him, he heard a sound and turned to see Ash brandishing a thick tree branch. The last thing Dusty remembered was feeling a heavy blow to his head as he crumpled to the ground with a thump.

Ash felt the blood from his brother's head spatter onto his shirt and looked down at Dusty as if he were a stranger. Ash quickly covered the car and his brother's body with tree branches and tall grasses so that they would not be discovered, then he disappeared into the woods.

Chapter Ten

Oh, Where Have All the Millers Gone?

usty lay unconscious all night. The next morning, he moved slightly and his eyes opened for a moment. He felt like he was slipping into another place—death, he imagined. His head was badly wounded and covered in dried blood. He pulled Penny Boy's note out of his pocket and held it tightly in his hands, as if this insignificant scrap of paper were somehow keeping him alive, then drifted back into blackness.

Penny Boy kept the box of seeds and the newly found green book close to him and waited by the waterfall for two days, but no Dusty came to get him. The robin, with the bell necklace, stayed nearby, hopping back and forth from a tree branch to the log. Penny Boy decided to open the metal box and sprinkle a handful of the rose seeds for the robin to eat, which it did with relish. Dusty would have done the same, he was certain.

The robin missed a few of the seeds, now wet from the rain that had begun falling.

Holding the metal box and the book under his shirt to keep them dry, Penny Boy slowly walked back toward the house, all the while hoping that Ash wouldn't find him. From the edge of the woods, he saw that Mr. and Mrs. Miller and Princess Cookie had returned with a truckload of new things.

Unnoticed, he slipped into the greenhouse and looked again upon the destruction—Dusty's prized and beautiful roses lying cut and torn all over the greenhouse floor. Penny Boy just couldn't fathom how anyone could do this; he simply had no frame of reference for the kind of evil person that Ash had become.

All the rest of that day and night, he hid in the greenhouse; no one came to look for him. He sensed that something terrible had happened to Dusty.

In the morning, Mrs. Miller whipped open the greenhouse door and stood staring in seeming shock at what lay before her. She spied Penny Boy cowering behind a turned-over bench. "What have you done, you horrible monster? What have you done to my things?" she screamed. She looked around at the broken windows, the roses on the floor, and the overturned pots; just like the furniture and windows in the house. She came running at Penny Boy with her arms outstretched toward him, her eyes ablaze with vengeance. Grabbing Penny Boy by the shirt, she demanded to know why he had done this. She shook him viciously as she accused him.

"You wrecked my beautiful things! And what have you done with Ash and Dusty? I'll show you what happens to bad, ugly creatures like you!" She dragged Penny Boy to the front door of the house, where Mr. Miller and a man named Crawley (who often came by to sell the Miller things and made a lot of money in the bargain) heard the commotion and came out of the library into the entrance hall.

"Never you mind," Harriet Miller yelled at them, "just go back to your business, Harold. I have this under control."

As the boy was being dragged past them, Mr. Miller was holding his notebook full of inventory, together with a big handful of cash to purchase things from Mr. Crawley's always-interesting collection. Harold Miller caught site of the green book in Penny Boy's hand at the same time Mr. Crawley did. "What's this?" they exclaimed simultaneously, both reaching out for the book, and Mr. Miller managed to snatch it out of Penny Boy's hand first.

"Ah, this looks old," he said, trying too obviously not to show his excitement at what he suspected was a valuable find.

"And perhaps even worth something," said Mr. Crawley, as nonchalantly as humanly possible, given the degree of his anxiety to get his hands on the book. "I know about these antiquities and can authenticate its value, Miller; let me have a look."

But Harold Miller kept a tight grip on it. They examined the cover carefully and stroked the mysteriously unfamiliar symbol on the front. When Mr. Miller opened it, his voice betrayed his great interest: "Yes, yes, Crawley, we may indeed have something here. Look at this, Harriet!" he yelled to his wife, now near the end of the hall and almost to the kitchen, dragging the boy along.

"Not now, Mr. Miller. I have had enough of this one! I can get rid of 'it,' finally!" She was pulling Penny Boy by his shirt into the kitchen. "Good news, though, about the book; sell it so we can pay for all the damage this monster did. Better yet, we can replace everything! Oh, how perfect! See how things always work out for us?" she yelled to him, chuckling.

Mr. Miller didn't really hear anything she said, though; he was too fascinated by the book to be distracted by her ramblings about Penny Boy and his shenanigans. He continued to pore over the book as Mr. Crawley stood next to him; then the pair disappeared into the library, jabbering about the possibilities of its value. "It looks authentic, doesn't it?" Harold asked Mr. Crawley.

"Very," the man replied, as he watched through the open library door the new cleaning woman scrubbing the entrance hall walls. There was something really peculiar about what she was trying to remove from them. "Do you hear something?" he asked Mr. Miller. "Is that a noise coming from those walls?"

Harold Miller was too engrossed in the book to hear him.

Meanwhile, Mrs. Miller dragged Penny Boy through the kitchen to a big wooden cupboard against the wall. With all her might and rage, she pushed on the heavy fixture with her body, grimacing and grunting and turning bright red in the face with the effort—all the while holding onto Penny Boy. Glasses, cups, dishes, and bowls all crashed to the floor as the shelves tilted, but she paid them no heed. *A good excuse to buy new ones,* she reasoned, as if she needed an excuse to buy anything.

Behind the cupboard there was a door, and as she opened it, stale air, reeking with the odor of mildew and mold, flooded into the room. Through the portal were steep stairs descending to a hallway. She pulled Penny Boy down the stairs and along the dark passage, at the end of which she stopped at a little, round, metal door. It looked like the kind that would be on a submarine, and its hinges screamed from many years of rust when she managed to swing it open. Pulling hard at Penny Boy, she dragged him toward the opening. Penny Boy held tightly to the metal box; nothing would make him let go.

Not caring about having what she presumed to be a worthless container, Mrs. Miller pushed the little coin-headed boy, box and all, through the door and watched him drop down more than ten feet into a square storage room of some kind; he hit the floor hard. A normal person might have broken some bones from such a fall, but, then, Penny Boy was anything but normal. Mrs. Miller slammed the door closed with a satisfied grunt and retraced her steps.

From a small, dirty, cracked window high above the floor of Penny Boy's new prison, a smattering of light made its way into the space. A surprised spider took notice of its new roommate for a few seconds, and then went back to the serious business of spinning a web.

About a half an hour later, the round door squeaked open again. Mrs. Miller threw all of Penny Boy's meager possessions down onto him, mostly things that Dusty had given him: a blanket, pencils and paper, a stuffed animal, a box of books, a baseball—worthless castoffs, by and large, but priceless treasures to Penny Boy.

"Good riddance, you little monster. Rot in there like the trash you are!" she yelled down and slammed the door shut again. This time, she pushed the big wooden cupboard back in front of the secret door in the kitchen. "So much for that!" she said smugly to herself, rubbing her hands together as she walked quickly away.

"Harriet," Harold called out, "this book will be quite useful Mr. Crawley told me. We will be able to replace everything here and even buy more than before. He'll be back in a few days to buy it. See how things work out for us?" he chuckled. *Smart move, very smart move, Mr. Miller!* he silently congratulated himself.

"Harold," Harriet replied, "I have a better plan. With that money, we can finally move from this wretched little wet place and go back to the city. Let's just leave it all right here and buy new things! We'll start fresh . . . forget this horrid place!"

Princess Cookie squeaked in her arms. "Oh, but of course not you, Princess Cookie. I couldn't forget you."

She kissed her little dog on the head. "How about a batch of butter cookies before we go to bed, Princess?" she cooed, then made her way to the kitchen.

"Tomorrow I'm gonna get the gardener to pull that coin off Penny Boy's head; it must have some value, Mr. Miller," she called out, but he was busy looking at the green book.

"Yes, indeed, Mr. Miller; this little item is worth a lot of money," he proudly mumbled to himself. "This is your lucky day!"

When Mr. Crawley returned in a few days with the money to buy the book, the Millers were nowhere to be found. The house was left wide open, with all the broken furniture and windows just as he had left them on his last visit. Mr. Crawley walked in through the front door and on into the library, but the old green book was not there. He searched the house from attic to basement but to no avail. Of course, he didn't find the secret door in the kitchen, so Penny Boy remained entombed in the dungeon where Mrs. Miller had thrown him.

As he walked through the empty house, Mr. Crawley became increasingly aware of snarling, growling, and scratching sounds coming from the blackened walls. His uneasiness soon turned to panic when he brushed lightly against one of the walls and had the distinct—and hair-raising—sensation of being touched. Only his greedy lust for the book could, temporarily, overcome his fear as he continued to search.

That changed quickly enough, however, when he entered the garishly decorated parlor and was confronted with the oil portrait of the Millers (holding that yappy dog, of course!) over the fireplace. Their saccharine smiles had become open-mouthed howls of pain, and he could swear that their arms seemed to be reaching out for him from the now grotesque and slimy canvas. He tore past the portrait and ran screaming in stark terror from the haunted mansion. In later years (after his release from the asylum), Mr. Crawley would repeat this story—to all within earshot and usually after a few too many drinks—about what a miracle it was that he had escaped with his life.

Unfortunately for them, however, the Millers and Princess Cookie had not been so lucky.

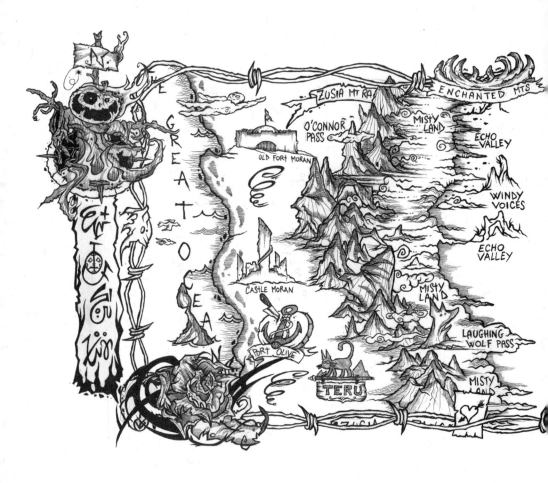

VALLEY OF THE GIANTS
THE GREAT FOREST
YAWNING RABBIT RIVER
OLD MILLER HOUSE
JACK TURNER HOUSE
JUMPING GRACE FALLS
BRIARWOOD INN
BRIDGE
BEGLEY FARM
BRIARWOOD

Part III
(Twenty Years Later)

Nub and Nil and the Yawning Rabbit River

Chapter Eleven

Autumn in the Valley

The Begley Farm was not far from the town of Briarwood, and it was located up the long gravel road that led into the quiet valley. Large flocks of curly horned blackface sheep grazed in the glen and on the sloping grassy pastures, hills, and steep mountains that made up the family farm. Apple trees, laden with golden pippins now ready for picking, grew all around the farmhouse as the autumn leaves in the surrounding forest turned shades of red, yellow, and purple.

At night, Nub Begley, the farmer's son, would sit outside on the farmhouse roof—something he loved to do when the weather was pleasant—and read his favorite books, *The Adventures of Kurt Burning Trail,* by the light cast from his bedroom window. Always present was the sound of the bubbling water of the nearby Yawning Rabbit River that ran down the middle of the valley from the untamed land to the north.

In the morning, like most mornings all year round, rain or shine—after breakfast and after his barn chores—Nub would

hurry down the dewy, grassy path to the river. He was a tall, lanky, dark-haired, thirteen-year-old boy who wore pants with patches and often went barefooted.

This morning, after getting his fishing pole from behind the big, yellowing weeping willow tree that drooped over the river, Nub jumped several feet across the running water to his favorite smooth, flat rock. Nub wasn't the only fisherman today; a red fox sat on the other side of the riverbank staring into the water, seeming not to take much notice of Nub's arrival—although you could be certain that it had. Just then, a great blue heron soared low over the water's surface, coming in for a landing.

With an almost silent "swoosh" of its gigantic wings, and with "landing gear" fully extended and angled slightly forward, the graceful bird settled easily into the shallow part of the river not far from Nub's position on "his" rock. Standing fully erect upon stilt-like legs, the blue-grey crane began peering keenly into the water.

"Ah, it must be breakfast time, Wizard Prince Ali Jau," Nub uttered quietly. He had given the bird that name and title because its appearance and personality reminded him of royalty and magic. "You're like a noble prince from another world," he had once told the bird.

Today, they would have new company, for a turtle with unusual green and yellow markings on its shell had positioned itself nearby and was now sitting in the mud watching. Suddenly aware of the presence of this unexpected guest, Nub looked down and said, "Hey, turtle, where'd you come from?"

Its slender neck stretched upward, seeming to look at the boy as if in quizzical response.

Dumb question, Nub thought. *Obviously, the river. Where else?*

Nub, the turtle, and the fox, each from his own vantage point, watched the slow, deliberate moves of the great blue heron moving effortlessly through the water, like some kind of tai chi master. Every now and then, its improbably long neck would duck into the water and immediately bob back up with some morsel of breakfast. *No need for a fishing pole there,* Nub thought.

Nub heard the eight-fifteen train whistle blow in the distance. "Uh, oh! Gotta run!" he muttered to the crowd. Hopping from the rock, he stood his fishing pole behind the willow tree and picked up his lunch bag. With a wave to the Wizard Prince and a "See ya!" to the turtle and fox, he hurried down the path and took his secret shortcut to school: across the big field of white autumn daisies to the road; then, down the road to Briarwood; and then over the fence to the schoolyard. *Piece of cake!* he chuckled silently to himself, feeling very proud of, yet again, making it to school on time. It was obvious that this was not the first time that the river had distracted him from his formal education.

Nub made it into his seat just as the bell rang, and he had only a moment to look around at the half-empty classroom. It seemed that there were fewer and fewer children coming to school every day.

Across from Nub sat the new girl, Nil Turner, who had just slipped into her chair, too. Her cheeks were rosy, and her long brown hair hung freely down her back.

No one really knew much about her except that she had come to Briarwood for summer vacation with her grandfather, Jack Turner. When summer ended, she had stayed on to attend the Briarwood school, and Nub was certainly glad she had.

Paying extra attention to Nil caused him to notice that the small, quiet girl carried a white ball with her every day. It was the kind of toy one would bounce in the playground or play word games with, like Alphabet Ball, but Nil just carried it around. And not just "carried it" but protected it, as if it were something important. *Very curious,* Nub thought.

Nil smiled at him as he watched her.

Nub smiled back.

"Nub!" called the teacher for the third time, trying to take attendance. "Nub!"

"Oh, yeah; here, Mrs. Dugan," he answered, quickly turning his head away from Nil and adjusting himself in his seat to face the front of the classroom. Just at that moment, George Melon, a boy with straw-colored hair and a shiny, round, pink face that matched his name, whirled around and aimed a spitball in Nub's direction. It missed and stuck in Nil's hair.

"You shouldn't have done that," Nil scolded George, pulling the wet glob from her hair.

"Yeah? Who's gonna stop me? You?" He just laughed and nervously scratched at the ugly zits covering his face. He was always picking them, so they never had a chance to heal.

"No, I'm not, but you will," she replied, with an air of confidence, exactitude, and a hint of mystery.

"I will what?" he questioned her. He waited for a reply, but none came. "I will what?" he asked again, nervous now and clearly agitated and concerned that maybe this time he had gone too far. George, like most bullies, could dish it out— usually to the smaller boys in the class and the girls—but he'd fold like wet paper if you really stood up to him. *Maybe she's got an older brother bigger than me,* he thought. *Heck, she wasn't my target, anyway!*

Nil still didn't answer but just looked at him, eye to eye, which made him even more uncomfortable and certain that he was in big trouble. Turning from pink to red, he just looked down at the floor and scratched at his face even more.

Nil couldn't help but notice how much George's head really did resemble a watermelon, and to make matters worse, he kind of smelled sour, like fruit rotting in the field. *What an appropriate family name he has!* she thought.

George shifted his gaze up from the floor and glanced over at Nub. "And what are you lookin' at?" he spluttered as menacingly as he could under such embarrassing circumstances.

Nub just ignored him. He could have given him the classic "Not much!" response, but he didn't have the heart to kick a guy this far down, even if George deserved it.

Disgusted and defeated, George turned around in his seat, flustered and red-faced and at a loss for words. Nil was correct; he had stopped himself, and it was the first time that the teacher didn't have to do it with a stern, "George Melon, for the *fiftieth* time; turn around! Pay attention in class! Do I have to take you to the office again?"

For Nub, the school day went by in its usual not particularly interesting way, except, of course, for Nil Turner. *She really does brighten up a room*, he thought to himself. *Why, she almost makes coming to school something to look forward to.* And fortunately for everyone, George Melon was unusually subdued for the rest of the day.

It wasn't so much that Nub was a bad student, for everyone agreed that he was bright enough . . . maybe even gifted. It was just that he didn't seem to apply himself to the business of acquiring a formal education. His parents used to spend a lot of time fretting about what to do with him, and they had many a discussion over the years with his teachers. Finally, they all just seemed to agree that there was nothing wrong with Nub, that maybe he was just bored with school, and that he was a little different.

As soon as the final bell rang for dismissal, Nub hopped the fence and ran back through the big daisy field toward the river. Before getting his fishing pole, he jumped onto his favorite rock to see if any fish were lurking about to be caught. Looking down, he was surprised to see the turtle still sitting there in the mud.

"Hey, what have you got there?" he said to it, leaping from the rock back to the riverbank for a closer look at the white autumn daisies in its mouth. He laughed. "You like daisies, huh? Should I call you 'Daisy'?"

A half hour passed as the turtle watched the boy cast the fishing line back and forth, over and over again—just for fun, as it turned out, because the fish weren't biting today. It didn't really matter to Nub; as with most true anglers everywhere in the world, his joy in fishing had very little to do with actually catching anything.

The distant sound of Tobia's incessant barking finally roused Nub from his daydreaming. The black and white border collie on the Begley Farm was not only his best friend but a very reliable clock as well, and Nub was being reminded that it was time to get back to work. "One of the smartest sheep dogs I ever saw," Nub's father, Francis Begley, would say. And it was true.

Nub put his fishing pole behind the willow and was off to the farm to do the afternoon chores. And he had to finish before it got too dark, because this evening, he had decided, would be a good time to pick the first of the pumpkins in the field by the light of the full harvest moon and carve them for his pumpkin-stand collection.

Chapter Twelve

Song for the River Goddess

Later, as Nub labored away in the pumpkin patch with Tobia by his side, Jack Turner, farther up river, stood on the edge of the deep pool of water beneath Jumping Grace Falls. Nil sat a little distance away with her pet rabbit, White Rice, curled up on her lap, anticipating what would happen next.

Out from under his grey wool poncho, Jack took out a small flute, a pennywhistle as it was commonly known, and began to play with fast, delicate, intricate skill. Nil was the lucky

audience—along with a tribe of tattooed melon heads—to attend this special occasion. Melon heads were plant-like creatures that, like fairies, were rarely visible to anyone except the people they chose to let see them. They came from the grassy fields in the untamed northern land and most likely were descendants of the grass goblins.

As Jack played, the melon heads arrived, one by one, cascading over the falls and plopping into the pool below. They

splashed into the water and climbed onto the rocks, all the while encouraging him with a constant barrage of, "Play us a song! Play us a song, Jack Turner!" Nil could barely contain her delight.

Suddenly, with a swirl in the center of the pool followed by a great splash, a golden river carp leaped from the water several times, as if on auspicious cue.

Jack Turner's flute sounds changed to a haunting, slower melody. The melon heads quieted down.

An orange glow was building in the lower half of the darkening violet-blue sky, and a full moon rose above the waterfall as if a theatre's stage lights were being slowly illuminated for a performance. With perfect timing, the water began churning as the legendary Dead Man Blues River Band slowly rose from the bottom of the river. It seemed as if the platform were mounted on hydraulic lifts, but there were no mechanical contraptions involved here. This was true river magic, and Jack Turner was the only living musician who had ever played with these spirit men of the Yawning Rabbit River.

At first, a slow drumbeat began, like the river's own rhythmic heartbeat; the drummer, Teddy "The Prophet" Sticks, was in no hurry. Then, the saxophone player, Mad-Dog Ollie, joined in with a sound so beautiful, you would just have to listen with your eyes closed. In time, like bird's wings delicately fluttering over the keys, Little John, the piano man, followed. Zachary Lee Bones began to pick his guitar strings.

With his captivatingly smooth voice, like he was calling out to the river goddess herself, Zachary began to sing an old river song, "The River Goddess Blues":

Oh, the river
runs through all kinds of places,
through the broken hearts,
past the lonely sad faces.

Man, the river, she is made of tears
of joy and pain,
carried in the silver clouds
filled with soothing rain.

Listen to her roll
'round rocks and trees.
Listen to her voice
sweeter than the breeze.

Tonight, tonight,
feel her gentle touch.
Tonight, tonight,
we need her so much.

Awaken by her side
from your murky sleep,
to the comfort
of her watery keep.

This river is like life,
it never ends,
but on her heartbeat
the river depends.

He sang it a second time, then again; by the third time, the melon heads were as quiet as babies after a lullaby—all of them blissfully sprawled out on the rocks and along the riverbank.

Hopefully, tonight the magic of the music will help, Jack Turner thought, as he continued playing.

They needed help, for Briarwood was terribly troubled.

Over the years, the charming town had grown up from a small river village. It even had a beautiful bronze-rabbit fountain in the town center, a tranquil place where people used to meet to sit and talk about their idyllic lives. That didn't happen anymore, not since the trouble started. Now, the local people spoke in frightened whispers, calling Briarwood Hospital the "house of the zombies." Beds were filling up with pitiable men, women, and children—turned pale grey, bewildered, and vacant of memory, with ashes falling out of their ears.

Each day, more and more of the townspeople fell victim to whatever horrible disease this was that had come to plague Briarwood.

Tonight, with the aid of the wind, the sound of the music traveled for miles—all the way to the Begley farm. Nub stopped his picking and stood straight up in the pumpkin field to listen.

At that same time, someone else was hearing it too: Penny Boy. The melody traveled over the treetops to the hilltop, then down the deserted dirt road to the entrance of the long sloping driveway of the Miller estate. It was barely distinguishable anymore, covered with two decades worth of leaves and debris and blocked by fallen tree limbs. The property was completely overgrown: giant wild ferns and tall grasses coated the ground; thick, dark green ivy vines twisted around the trees and up the sides of the big house, creeping their way inside through the many broken windows.

Inside, as if it were an amusement park, field mice and chipmunks raced along the echoing hallways, across the marble kitchen countertops, and over the elaborate appliances left by Mrs. Miller. Occasionally, a luckless squirrel or two would wander into the derelict mansion in search of a nice nesting spot out of the weather and would never be seen again. At such times, one could almost hear a sigh and commotion coming from the disgusting black walls.

Next to the dwelling, the small greenhouse Dusty had built remained, although partially collapsed. Broken flowerpots lay scattered about on the floor where they had fallen after Ash's violent destruction.

Amidst a thick coating of dust that covered everything, Penny Boy sat entombed beneath the mansion's kitchen in the hidden room into which the cruel Mrs. Miller had tossed him. Alone, day after day, night after night, year after year, his only company in this dungeon had been the spider, whose secret

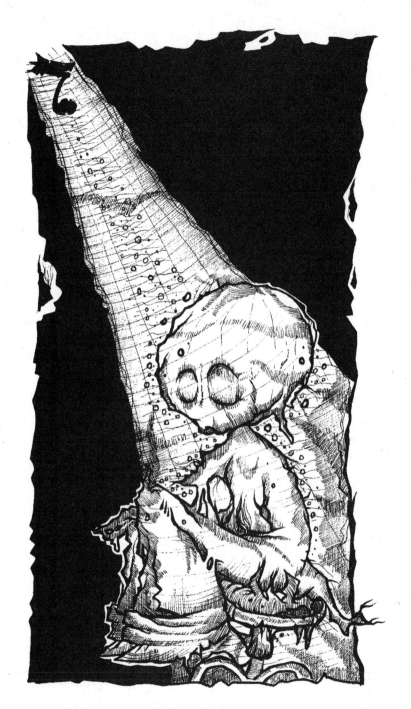

space he had been forced to invade. Penny Boy's sole distraction from a numbing existence had been watching the spider spin her web, but that, too, had ended with the spider's death from old age. Penny Boy, who didn't—couldn't—age at all, was completely alone. But tonight, for the first time in many years, this sweet, beautiful sound, this music from the river, penetrated its way through the crack in the window glass high above Penny Boy's prison. He was "alone" no longer, the music told him.

Chapter Thirteen

A Troubled Town

Early the next morning, Nub awoke to the familiar engine hum of John O'Connor's truck coming down the driveway, then turning toward one of the barns. He was a good friend of Nub's dad. Looking out the window, Nub saw a soft, thin rain falling on the lush, emerald-green landscape.

Nub dressed in his usual "style"—patched-up blue jeans, faded checkered shirt, work boots—and went down to the kitchen. The wood in the fireplace was just a red glow of coals, and all was quiet in the farmhouse. For breakfast, he cut himself a piece of apple cake and poured a glass of milk. On the table, his lunch bag for school was waiting for him.

At the barn, Nub led the four farm horses—Old Tom, Sienna, Jimbo, and Rudy—into the big grass paddock one at a time and closed the gate. Although he didn't know it, the bloodline of these animals went all the way back to Meeka and Mercury, the horses from the Great Forest. After mucking out their stalls and filling the feed and water tubs, Nub checked the firewood pile to make sure that there was plenty of wood for that day and the next. Early chores completed, he hurried to the river, leaping over the rain puddles as if springs were in his feet.

Having quickly retrieved his pole from the willow-tree hiding spot, he took his position on his favorite rock and cast his line into the river. Right away, he felt a tug on the line. *Fishin's always better when it's raining,* he thought excitedly, anticipating a quick catch. But then there was nothing, and the line went limp. Larger raindrops began to fall, making holes in the water like dimples. Fallen leaves floated on the surface, catching in the line. As he picked off the leaves, Nub heard the sound of his friend's large flapping wings.

"Frauhwk, frauhwk, frauhwk!" the Wizard Prince called out, gliding just inches above the water before landing.

Nub watched the heron dip his handsome head under the clear water and come up with a spotted brown trout in his beak. With a quick, acrobatic "gulp," breakfast was over.

Between his fishing and lazily watching the river pass by, Nub, as usual, completely lost track of the time, and it was quite a while after the train whistle blew before he left the riverbank.

The morning bell had already rung, but as luck would have it, Mrs. Dugan was engrossed in the morning newspaper and hadn't called attendance yet. Nub, deftly hopping over the leg that George had extended into the aisle to trip him, slid noiselessly and unobserved into his seat. He was sorry to see that Nil's seat was empty.

George turned to Nub, looking him up and down, and yelled loudly, "It's raining out, idiot!" With a glance at the floor, he exclaimed, "Uh, Mrs. Dugan, Nub is making a puddle on the floor!" He pointed and laughed mockingly.

Mrs. Dugan briefly looked up from the newspaper. "Georgie Melon! For the fiftieth time, turn around!" Then she went right back to what she had been reading. She seemed upset and—very uncharacteristically—not at all interested in George's antics or anything else.

George hated it when the teacher called him "Georgie" in front of the class, especially in front of Nub. *It's humiliating*, he thought, making a mental note to get even with Nub at the first opportunity.

It was still raining at lunchtime, and as Nub walked past the teacher's desk, he saw the headlines of the morning newspaper: ENTIRE FAMILIES STRICKEN! it read, in gigantic type. No wonder Mrs. Dugan was upset; no doubt some of the children were her students, and she would have known the parents.

In town, near the rabbit fountain outside Joe's Coffee Shop, a group of people had gathered in the rain under their open umbrellas. Frank Jones, owner of the Briarwood Inn, held up the morning news-

paper. "Have you read this?" he exclaimed. "The Bruno family can't even remember their own names!"

"Oh, it's horrible!" Mary Burns added. "Little grey ashes are coming out of their ears. What a terrible disease."

"That Bruno family didn't use umbrellas, did they? They lived close by the river too, right?" questioned a man with a ruddy-red, round face. He was wearing dark-tinted glasses, a black suit, black raincoat, black hat, and black tie, and he carried a black umbrella.

"And who are you?" asked Frank Jones, not recognizing what little he could see of the stranger's face in all that cloak-and-dagger clothing.

"I'm here to investigate some things; name's Devlin . . . Detective Mike Devlin," he told them. He flashed a shiny, official-looking badge and quickly returned it to his pocket. No one really had a chance to take a close look at it, much less read what was on it, but he didn't seem to be the kind of person you'd want to openly doubt.

The group went quiet with unease and stared at the stranger nervously.

"Yes, they live by the river. I don't know if they used umbrellas or not. What does that have to do with anything?" Mary responded, puzzled by the presence of this investigator in their town.

"Hey, that don't mean anything 'round here, mister," said Frank Jones.

"Mmm . . . uh, you sure about that?" the stranger continued. "They didn't use an umbrella. I already checked into it."

"So why'd you ask then?" said Frank Jones.

All eyes were on the man.

"Well," muttered Devlin, in a low tone, "have you noticed it's been the no-umbrella people who live mostly by the river?

And it's the no-umbrella people who have been attacked. Why do you think that is?"

Frank was quick to answer. "Listen, buddy, my inn is by the river, and I have an umbrella right here in my hand, as you can plainly see. So there goes your smart-alecky theory about—"

"Do you have any no-umbrella people staying there?" the detective abruptly interrupted.

"You got some nerve, man!" responded Frank, clearly outraged by the insinuation that he might be involved in some way with this weird Bruno family business. "You tryin' to stir up more trouble than this poor town already has?"

"What are you saying?" chimed in Mary Burns. "That the disease is their fault . . . or the river's fault? Do you think the no-umbrella people are making it dangerous for us?"

"Hey, I'm just tryin' to look out for you good umbrella people! If you ask me, I don't think it's a very good idea to have them no-umbrella folks at your inn, Mr. Jones." That one statement revealed that Devlin already knew Jones's name and what he did for a living—so he probably had everybody else's information as well. "It's risky," Devlin added. "Just askin' for trouble with *that* kind."

Frank Jones held his head down, shaking it back and forth. When he did look up, his face was flushed. "Well, then, I'll make it simple for ya, Mr. Deee-tec-tive: I didn't ask you! And anyway, I'm sure that isn't even the case; just a coincidence, I'd say."

"Yeah, but isn't it odd that *they* have been the only ones attacked by this disease?" piped up the coffee shop owner, Joe Pyeweed. Having noticed the gathering outside his shop, he had come out to find out what was going on. "Maybe you *should* be more careful, Frank. Makes me wonder about things, you know what I mean?" he added softly, glancing back through the shop window at the counter customers, some with wet clothes because they didn't use umbrellas.

"No, Joe, I don't," Frank answered. He lived close by the river and had built the inn there because he loved the place. He figured others would like the beautiful spot as well and that the inn would become prosperous. The fact was, he actually preferred *not* to use an umbrella, because he enjoyed the rain. He carried one mostly to fit in—and fitting in made good business sense.

You see, Briarwood had two kinds of people: those who carried umbrellas, the "umbrella" type, and those who didn't, the "no-umbrella" type. Once, in the *Briarwood Times*, a spokesperson for the no-umbrella people had told a reporter: "The rain just is; it doesn't occur to us to not get wet. We rather enjoy it. Why is that so difficult to understand?" And with a laugh, had added, "The Yawning Rabbit River doesn't mind being all wet, so why should we?"

In the same article, a spokesperson for the people who used umbrellas said, "It's just not natural not to have an umbrella. Why would anyone want to get all wet in the rain? Of course the Yawning Rabbit River is already wet. It's water! Saying it 'doesn't mind' is ridiculous. There's no logic in that. A person could come down with an awful cold or flu from being wet. It just doesn't seem right or make any sense to not use an umbrella!"

As he did for every coffee break, Police Chief Chester Dugan had gone to the coffee shop. He was sitting at a table by the window, eating from a tall stack of his favorite sugared donuts. Draining the last of the coffee in his big mug, he put the remaining few donuts in a bag to save them for an after-

noon snack. As he walked out of the coffee shop, he snapped open his umbrella.

"What do you think about this, chief?" asked Joe, spotting Dugan coming out. "Why is it that just no-umbrella people have been stricken by this awful disease? Maybe you should do something about it."

"Yeah, yeah; I heard Devlin's theory earlier this morning, when he came snoopin' around the station," the chief answered. "So what do you think should be done, Joe? Do you want me to go house to house searching for umbrellas? And then what; ask 'em to leave town if I don't find one?"

"Maybe," said Joe, defensively. "This thing kind of puts all of *us* in danger, don't ya' think? And what about our businesses?"

"Umbrella, no-umbrella . . . don't matter; you can be sure of that," came a voice from behind the group. The handsome Jack Turner was speaking. "What's it in for you?" he asked Detective Devlin directly. "That's a dangerous accusation you're making. No-umbrella people just happen to live down by the river, which is mostly where this has been happening for now, that's all. It's more a matter of geography not philosophy," Jack added in a serious, assured tone.

"Oh, Mr. Devlin was just telling us his theory about who has been attacked by the terrible disease," Mary Burns explained, trying to smooth things over.

"Ah, so it's just a theory, is it? Well, that certainly makes all the difference in the world then," Jack said sarcastically. "I don't think your theory holds much water, if you'll pardon the pun." With that, Jack looked directly at Devlin with his piercing blue eyes. "What's in it for you?" he asked again.

"Hey, nothin's in it for me, mister!" Devlin shot back. "I've been sent here to investigate this. I gotta ask questions!" He took out his shiny badge again and held it up. "Like I said, my name's Mike Devlin . . . Detective Mike Devlin. What's your name?"

Jack Turner looked at Devlin and studied him through squinted eyes. After a moment of silence, he asked, "Sent here by whom?"

"Uh, by the agency, of course," Devlin replied, a bit too defensively.

"The 'agency,' huh? Yeah, right!" Jack Turner shook his head. "Maybe you should go ask the river, mister! I think you might find what you're lookin' for there!"

"And what exactly am I lookin' for?" Devlin barked back.

But Jack Turner had turned around and was walking away in the rain—without an umbrella. "Time will tell, time will tell," he called out over his shoulder. "It always does!" His long, dark-brown hair, face, and gray poncho were soaking wet. From his side pocket he took his flute and began to play a cheerful melody, as if rain and music go together—which, of course, they do.

"That's Jack Turner," Mary Burns informed Detective Devlin. "He's quite remarkable really, so charming."

"Oh, yeah? Remarkable and charming, is he? Why's that? He ain't got no umbrella!"

"Oh, he wouldn't think of it! People say his music is enchanting, and they swear it brings them good luck, too."

"Aha, so he's a good-luck maker, huh? Just a lot of hocus-pocus malarkey!" replied Devlin mockingly. "Ain't no such thing, lady!"

"But he's simply marvelous with the pennywhistle. Just listen," Mary said and closed her eyes to concentrate on the fading notes as Jack disappeared from sight.

"Hmm, let's see now . . . don't use an umbrella," Devlin repeated, taking out his little notebook and writing it down. "Calls himself 'Jack Turner.' And he lives down by the river, right? Just like the rest of 'em," he added, scribbling it all down.

"Well, yes," said Mary, "but . . ."

"Yep," confirmed Devlin and wrote something else in his notebook. "Better look into this," he mumbled under his breath. "What's his address? I'll need all yours, too," he said to the group. "I'll be needing to come to your homes to look around a bit, so just letting you know now, good people.

Okay, let's start with you," he said, looking directly at Joe Pyeweed.

Seeming a bit surprised and uncomfortable, Joe glanced around at the crowd of people holding up their umbrellas, all kind of trying not to look at him or each other. "Well, I guess if you're a detective here to help," said Joe, nervously surrendering himself to this authority figure.

The rest of the group sheepishly followed suit and gave Devlin what he asked for. Even Mary Burns, who considered herself a good friend of Jack Turner's, didn't utter a peep of protest at this infringement of their civil rights.

Chapter Fourteen

An Afternoon of Surprises

eanwhile, during school lunch recess, Nub had decided to play outside in the rain. He walked along the fence rails, balancing himself with his arms outstretched and hopping over the posts. For some reason, George watched him from the window with great interest. He saw Nub glance toward the ground and then jump down.

"Daisy!" Nub called out as he kneeled next to the object. "Is that you?" Nub was amazed to see a brown turtle looking at him. It had the distinct yellow and green markings of the one he had seen by the river the day before. "How'd you get here?"

While Nub was talking to the turtle, George had snatched up his umbrella, rushed out of the classroom, and was running toward them.

"What's this . . . a friend of yours, no-umbrella boy?" George blurted out when he saw the creature. "Only a weirdo like you would talk to a turtle!" He made threatening movements to try to grab the turtle, but Nub blocked him.

"Get out of here, George!"

Just then, a strong gust of wind caught George's umbrella and wrenched it out of his hand. As it flew across the deserted yard away from the school, George felt the rain pelting his face and fled back to the classroom as if his life depended on it.

Nub knew that the turtle was not safe with George around, so he decided to return it to the river right away, even though the recess bell would ring soon. *Maybe I can make it back before Mrs. Dugan misses me*, he thought and snatched Daisy up. He tucked her under his arm for protection from the weather, then realized how silly that was. *Gee, like this turtle minds getting wet!* he chuckled to himself.

Racing from the schoolyard, he made record time back to the river and placed the turtle down on the mud near his favorite rock. He should have gone back to school, but he didn't. He was pretty soaked by now, and besides, Nil wasn't even there. He decided to just skip the rest of the day. Even fishing didn't seem to interest him, so he plopped down on his rock and watched the way the water moved in the rain and listened to the sounds it made.

The clouds parted revealing a patch of bright blue sky, and the sunlight shone through the glistening wet leaves over his head. Nub heard someone coming down the path.

"Hi, Nub," Nil called out cheerily. She was carrying the white ball and seemed both surprised and delighted to find him there.

"Hi, Nil!" Nub answered and quickly stood up. "You weren't at school today," he added.

"And how would you know that, playing hooky down here by the river?" she replied with a smile.

"Yeah, well, not exactly hooky, I was there . . . until lunch recess, at least; I found this turtle in the yard and . . . ," Nub looked down, but the turtle was gone. "Well, I found a turtle at school and brought it back to the river. George was trying to get it, so . . ."

"That was kind of you," Nil told him, hopping onto the rock with ease. She sat down and plopped the white ball into her lap, motioning Nub to sit next to her.

"So, how do you like it here?" he asked her. This was the first time Nub had been alone with Nil and could ask her about herself. "Well, I mean before the trouble started. Did you have a good summer with your grandfather?"

Nil nodded. "Yes, mostly, but the town is in trouble for sure."

"Is Briarwood similar to where you come from?" Nub asked, curious about her previous home. He thought he had noticed an accent in her voice, like she may have come from another state or country. "Is it far from here?"

Nil touched the water with her fingers. "No, not very."

Nub watched her. "Oh, I see. Well, where is it then?"

She didn't say anything.

"Did your grandfather give you that?" he asked, pointing to the white ball.

"No, my mother did," she answered. She looked at him and studied his face.

"What?" he smiled, wondering what she had on her mind.

"Can you keep a secret?" she asked.

"Sure I can!" he shot back, silently insulted that she even had to ask such a question. Nub crossed his heart in promise.

Satisfied, Nil leaned over, and with both hands, she dipped the white ball into the water, fully immersing it for a few seconds. When she brought the wet ball back to her lap, it quivered a bit, then slowly began to unravel itself. Right before his eyes, Nub watched the ball turn into a beautiful white rabbit with a brown patch over one eye. Nil picked it up and kissed its furry, two-tone face.

Nub couldn't believe what had just happened. "How'd you do that?" he asked, assuming that it must be some sort of magic trick. "Wow," he said, "you'd really be a big hit at the next talent show at school with that act!"

"It's *no* trick . . . although it's certainly magic! The river did it!" she exclaimed, handing the rabbit to Nub to examine. He felt for springs or other devices that might account for the transformation, but he could find no evidence that it was anything but a real, live, really cute rabbit. *Beats the heck out of me, that's for sure!* he had to silently admit.

"Her name is White Rice," Nil told him, reaching over to pet the soft creature's head and long ears.

Momentarily speechless (a rare condition for Nub), he continued holding onto the rabbit that was seconds ago an ordinary white ball. Not being able to stand it any longer, he blurted out again, "Aw, come on, Nil! How'd you do that?" He looked at her, then the rabbit, then at Nil again.

The girl just shrugged her shoulders.

"Your grandfather's a magician, right? Did he teach you that?"

Nil shook her head. "The river did it. It's a magic river."

"Yeah, right!" Nub replied. "Really, Nil, you can tell me. I'll keep your secret, I promise!"

He waited for her to say something, but she didn't. They both sat on the big rock together, watching the rabbit, then the river.

"Come on, where'd you live before?" Nub asked, trying to coax her into revealing some information about the rabbit.

Nil still didn't answer. It seemed that she didn't want to tell him anything more.

"You ever been in the circus?" Nub asked.

She rolled her eyes and laughed. "Nooo . . . !"

"Well, where then? You had to learn that trick somewhere! Can you teach me?"

Nil stood up without answering.

"Where're you going?" Nub asked.

"It's not a trick, and I didn't do it; the river did," she insisted.

"I've never seen the river do that before, and I've lived around it all my life. I know Jack Turner—I mean, your grandfather—is kind of . . . uh, well" (Nub searched for just the right word; he didn't want to antagonize Nil even more) "well . . . *different*, and I imagine you are, too." *Phew*, he thought, *that was a close one!*

She looked at him and smiled. "I guess you could say that . . ." she paused for a moment to compose her thoughts ". . . that this *river* is different, you know, from most rivers. I mean, it has a very interesting history, and there are all kinds of unusual things about it."

"Like what," he asked, "besides fish and turtles and the Wizard Prince?"

She giggled.

"Nub, have you ever heard how the Yawning Rabbit River got here and how it got its name?" Nil asked him.

Nub, still sitting and holding the rabbit, looked up at her. "I don't know . . . maybe. What do you mean? No, maybe I don't really know. Okay, how? How did it get here . . . and why that name? And just how do you know so much about it?"

"Jack Turner has an old book all about it," she told him. "Want to see it? It's at his house."

"Yeah!" Nub replied, excited by the prospect of sharing this confidence with Nil.

"Come on then," Nil told him, putting out her arms for the rabbit.

Nub held on to White Rice, stood up, then passed her back to Nil. She held the rabbit close and jumped off the rock over the water onto the ground. Nub followed. They walked down the path, crossed over the stone bridge past the Briarwood Inn, and continued on toward Jack Turner's place.

"You call your grandfather Jack Turner?" Nub questioned.

"Yes," was all she replied.

As they walked, Nil held White Rice in one hand and took Nub's hand with her other.

When they arrived, Nil opened the front door with a key on a string around her neck. "Jack Turner keeps the door locked," she explained. "I know nobody locks up around here, but this book is very special, and what with the trouble and all . . ."

Nub looked around as he stood in the entrance hallway. He had never been inside the house before. Nil went into the living room and put White Rice on a chair next to the book-case. Nub followed her into the room and looked at the book-shelves. Books of all colors and sizes filled the wooden shelves from floor to ceiling, wall to wall. "Gee," he said, "I'll bet there are more books here than the school library!"

"Could be," replied Nil, as she pulled a green-covered book from the middle of one of the shelves.

"You can't tell anyone about this book, okay?" she reminded him.

"Okay," he replied.

Nil held out the book for Nub to look at. On the cover, which was made of thick green cloth, there was a gold-embossed raised symbol, kind of like two half circles back to back with some writing and symbols around it. The book had no title. Nub ran his fingers over the cover. They tingled, and he yanked them away.

"Aha!" exclaimed Nil, excitedly. "You felt that! I thought you would. This book can cast a spell on someone if it wants to."

"Wow," Nub muttered. "No way!"

"Yes!" she laughed. "It can be quite serious."

He touched the symbol again, and again his fingers tingled slightly. It reminded him of what it feels like when a cat is purring and you have your hand on it. *Weird . . . really weird!* he thought.

"What kind of book is this?" he asked Nil.

"A history book, I guess you could call it, but not like most; it has lots of forgotten things from a long time ago. See the 'R. S.' written here on these pages?" she asked, pointing to the initials. "And here it is again: 'R. Snow.'"

Nub looked. "Yeah."

"That's the author," she added.

"Here," she said and handed the book to Nub. "It's about the river and the river goddess, named Violet. It's about her life and what happened to her. But, then, there's a lot more: about how a rabbit thief from these very woods found her and raced her for the river."

Nub looked over at White Rice, asleep on a chair.

Nil knew what he was thinking. "No, not her; the rabbit in this book is named Sean," she told him.

"You say he won the river in a race . . . this river? I don't understand. How can you *win* a river?" exclaimed Nub.

"Well, no, I guess you can't really win a river. He wanted to do it for love, and I guess the goddess thought that was a good reason and went along with it. It's kind of complicated," Nil added.

Nub laughed. "I'll bet! And I'm supposed to believe that this really happened?"

"Yep, it's all true, believe it or not," Nil said, giving poor Nub another of those smiles that melted away whatever resistance he had left. "See, look here at this poem." She leaned over and turned the pages while Nub held the book.

"It's here somewhere." She was turning the pages quickly, looking for the right place. "Ah, this is it. Here, Nub, read this poem."

Nub looked closely at the page and read it out loud slowly:

> "An opening to such a place
> of magic, love, and of grace,
> there's no such thing as a race
> to find or win such a river!

A heart that sings is the only key,
a heart of courage and humility;
on this matter trust in me
to find such a river!"

She looked at Nub and said, "See!"

Nub kept turning the pages, as if thumbing through the book would clarify its meaning somehow. "Well, how did Jack Turner get this book?"

"I'll tell you more tomorrow; I promise. Come back tomorrow to look at it more if you want. The book has to stay here, where it's safe."

"Okay, for sure," Nub answered. "I will."

A piece of paper fell out of the book and fluttered to the floor.

Nil picked it up and unfolded it. "Oh, this is the map Sean drew to find Violet."

Nub looked at it briefly, not recognizing any of the landmarks. "Sean, you say . . . a rabbit drew this? That's impossible!"

"No, it's not. You'll see. You can look at it more tomorrow," Nil told him and took the paper back. She folded it carefully and placed it back between the pages.

Nub closed the book and gave it back to her. "Nil, is this really true about the river?"

She laughed at his disbelief and then gave him a nod. "Yes, Nub, and it's not only true, but it's the most beautiful story of love and adventure you could ever imagine."

Walking to the door, he turned to say goodbye to Nil, now cradling White Rice in her arms. "Bye, Nil, see you tomorrow at school. Thank you for showing me the book."

"You're welcome, Nub. I'll see you tomorrow then," she said with a big smile. Her eyes twinkled.

Nub felt giddy walking back down the path to the bridge. All he could think about was Nil, and how much he liked her. This quiet new girl was full of surprises—and so was this day. He stopped in the middle of the bridge to look down at the river. *It's an incredible story*, he thought. *I can't wait to see Nil tomorrow.*

He was feeling light on his feet, and, once over the bridge, he ran down the path all the way to the farm. Tobia was waiting for him by the fence entrance and gave a huge bark when he came into sight. "Hey, boy! Wow, wait 'til I tell you about today! But you'll have to keep it quiet, cuz it's a secret."

Nub came in through the back door to the kitchen. He smelled apple pie baking in the oven and saw dinner on the table. Tobia hurried through the kitchen, past the table set for dinner, and on into the living room. Nub heard his mother talking with someone there.

"We're in here, Nub," he heard his mother call to him. When he walked in, he saw his father and mother standing and talking to a man with a pink round face. He was wearing a black hat and black raincoat and had a closed umbrella in his hand.

"This is my son, Nub, Mr. Devlin," Gina Begley told him.

"Nub, this is Mr. Devlin. He is here to investigate what's been happening."

Nub saw the look on his father's face. Francis Begley didn't talk much, and he didn't have to say a word now; his face said everything. He didn't like this guy.

"Oh?" replied Nub, looking at the man suspiciously.

"Hello, Nub," said Devlin, pretending not to notice the

cool reception he was getting. "And it's Detective Devlin," he added, flashing his official gold badge once more for Nub's sake.

"Hi," replied Nub flatly, Tobia at his side. Tobia's ears were laid back flat against his head—a thing he did when he felt threatened. "What's this all about?"

"Well, we're not sure what the devil is goin' on here," Devlin said, trying to sound concerned, but Nub didn't believe him. "Have you seen anything unusual lately, son?" he asked Nub, taking out his little notebook and pen.

Yeah, most definitely, Nub thought to himself. *I've seen lots of unusual things today, but I'm not tellin' you anything about any of it: a turtle that followed me to school, a girl with a magic rabbit, and an old book with a spell about the Yawning Rabbit River. Hmm, maybe it could put a spell on this joker!* Nub laughed to himself at that thought. "No, nothing really," he replied.

"Uh, huh. I see. 'No, nothing really,'" Devlin repeated Nub's words, looking wearily at him. He jotting down something in the little book, then looked around the room as if he really weren't interested in Nub's answer anyway but something else.

"Okay then, well, thank you for your time," Devlin said, once more looking around the room before he walked over to the door and opened it slowly.

"Looking for something?" Gina Begley asked him.

"Uhhhh, oh, no," the man replied awkwardly.

"Well, good night then," said Nub's father as he closed the door just a bit too firmly behind Devlin, obviously relieved to see the man leave.

"What a rude busybody!" exclaimed Mrs. Begley. "Guess that's why he's a nosey detective."

"Tobia doesn't like him, and neither do I," Nub added. "What a snoop!"

"I can think of a couple other things to say about him," said Francis, with a laugh. "Come on; let's forget about that guy and just enjoy our dinner!"

Chapter Fifteen

Pumpkins for Sale

he next morning was Friday. It was a sunny, crisp, cool day. After breakfast, while doing the barn chores, Nub thought the horses seemed restless and nervous. Nub and Tobia walked through the pumpkin patch to take further inventory and pick a few more that were ready. This year's pumpkin crop was a very good one. There were big, round, bright-orange pumpkins, tall thin ones, and perfect little pumpkins; all suitable for funny and scary cut-out faces.

"I'll fill the cart later and take the pumpkins to the stand right after school," Nub said out loud; Tobia understood. "Well, not right after." First, he would go see the green book with Nil and ask her to come to the pumpkin stand with him.

He walked back to the house, took his lunch bag off the kitchen table, and put it in his pack. He was off to the river for a quick visit. Not bothering to get his fishing pole today, he jumped to his rock and whistled. No red fox, but the Wizard Prince arrived, gliding in for a landing, then standing by the rock to peer into the water. Nub scanned the riverbank for the turtle, but there was no sign of Daisy.

"See ya' later Ali," Nub said to his friend the heron and leaped from the rock.

Nub slipped into his seat at school. The bell rang seconds later. Nil's seat was empty again. "Melon Head" George started to turn around, but before he could mutter a comment, Mrs. Dugan called out right on cue: "George Melon, for the fiftieth time, turn around!"

Nub couldn't be bothered with this nuisance today.

The morning subjects started; first math, then science, and then history. *But no subject can be more interesting than the history of the Yawning Rabbit River,* Nub thought.

Outside at lunch recess, Nub sat on the fence rail, feeling impatient to get the school day over with. It would be fun to have Nil's company and for her to meet Tobia. *Where is she,* he wondered? He couldn't wait to see her.

"Hey, Nub, look what I have here!" It was the diabolical voice of George.

Nub looked up. George was holding up the turtle in one hand, swinging it in the air by one of its legs! Nub leaped from the fence and rushed toward him.

"Give me the turtle, George!" he demanded.

George laughed and threw it in the air, catching it again but barely.

Nub had almost reached him.

George threw the turtle into the air for a second time. "Here!" he shouted and ran away.

"Daisy!" Nub called out. Before Nub could reach it, the turtle hit the ground with a *thump!* Nub quickly but carefully picked up the turtle. It seemed lifeless. Nub hoped it was just stunned by the fall. He examined the shell, and there weren't any cracks he could find, but the turtle wasn't moving. Its eyes were closed, and its head and four little legs hung limp.

Nub carried Daisy in his arms across the daisy field toward the river.

When he reached the riverbank near his fishing rock, he placed the turtle on the cool mud and waited. He cupped a little water from the river and sprinkled it over the turtle. Daisy didn't move. He thought about Doc Nearing, the veterinarian, but all he ever took care of was horses, cows, and sheep and once, Tobia. For an hour Nub stayed with the turtle, sitting on his rock, watching over it. He decided he would leave it hidden, and covering the turtle with fallen leaves for camouflage, he hoped for the best. He would check on Daisy first thing after he found Nil; maybe she could help. He headed toward Jack Turner's house.

When Nub arrived at the cottage, he knocked on the door. No one answered. He looked through the window into the entrance hall. The house was quiet. He could see the bookshelves across the room and the empty chair next to them. He tapped on the window, then knocked on the door again. He tried the doorknob. The door was locked. Putting his hand in his pocket, he found a small pencil and a piece of scrap paper. He wrote: *Nil, come by the pumpkin stand. It's important! Nub.* Then he drew a smiling pumpkin face below the words and put the note in the mail basket hanging next to the door.

He was ready to leave, but his curiosity was like a spell of its own. He looked through the window again, just to see if he could see the green book on the shelf. There it was! He knew he'd have to wait to see it another time.

On his way back to the farm, Nub planned to stop at the Briarwood Inn to ask the owner, Frank Jones, if he wanted any special cut-out pumpkins for the front steps, as he had ordered last year. Then he would check on the turtle as he passed by. Climbing up the stone steps to the inn that overlooked the river, Nub could smell something burning. It was possible that the inn's chef, Ted Sprinkle, was burning the pumpkin pies or the roasted duck, having drunk too much of the cooking wine again. He was an eccentric chef who practiced martial arts while cooking with his sharp kitchen knives and culinary forks; when he drank too much, it could be dangerous for any kitchen staff, bird, vegetable, or anything else that got in his way. He was a great chef, however, and had made the Briar-wood Inn very popular for its excellent food.

Nub heard a commotion and what sounded like scream-ing coming from around the back of the inn. Suddenly Ted Sprinkle, following a rolling pumpkin, charged toward Nub like a whirlwind.

"Nub! Nub! Run for your life!" screamed the chef. "A fiend!"

"Have you been drinking again, Chef Sprinkle?" Nub called out. "What friend?"

"No, Nub, not a friend, a fiend," the chef yelled back. The bald-headed man wearing his tall white chef's hat was now tangled with the pumpkin. They both tumbled down the hill in a great cluster and disappeared.

Nub sprinted up the steps, two at time, reaching the large porch; it was vacant, the row of red, wooden rocking chairs was empty. The front door was open. The main room was empty, and no one was at the reception desk. The smell of burning grew stronger. Nub used the phone at the desk to call the police.

He headed toward the kitchen and passed through the dining room, where plates full of food and cups of tea were left on the tables, and the chairs were knocked over. In the kitchen, pots were cooking on the stove, bubbling and spilling over. Nub turned them off. He saw a big butcher's knife on the chopping block and picked it up. Through the back window of the kitchen, he could see people lying on the back lawn as if they were dead. Nub hurried to the back steps but stopped when he saw a hunched-over figure in a long, torn, black coat. With a flaming hand, it had hold of Frank Jones. Frank saw Nub and screamed, "Run, Nub! Run!"

Nub yelled, "Hey!" He held the knife up in the air.

The creature looked at Nub, its sickly pale face covered with deep gashes and scars and with strange, crazed, dark eyes, circled in grey. It widened its eyes and straightened its spine. Dropping Frank Jones to the ground, it came quickly toward Nub.

Frank jumped to his feet and ran at the creature, jumping on its back, but the monster paid him no mind and kept moving toward the boy. Frank pounded on its back. "Nub! Run," Frank Jones yelled, but Nub just stood there. The creature approached the bottom step. It raised its flaming hand in the air and whined a high-pitched, horrible howl. Then, for no apparent reason, it turned and hurried back across the lawn. Frank Jones let go and fell to the ground. Then, hunched over, the monster disappeared into the thick woods behind the inn.

"I called the police and an ambulance," Nub told Mr. Jones. "What was that thing?"

"I don't know, but Briar-wood doesn't have a

disease problem; they have a monster problem," Frank Jones replied as they both hurried to the grey-colored victims. Some were lying face down, some face up, and some were wandering aimlessly around on the lawn. Their eyes were open, but they had no expressions on their faces, and ashes fell from their ears.

Nub and Frank heard the sirens of the police and ambulance as they arrived. Chief Chester Dugan and two other policemen came running around the back of the inn, followed by the first-aid team and the panicked Mrs. Jones. Frank and Nub explained to the police chief what they had seen as the first-aid volunteers put the grey people on stretchers; it was the first time anyone had witnessed what happened to these people.

"Like Frank Jones said, '*Briarwood has a monster problem*,'" Chief Dugan told the news reporter who arrived. That would be tomorrow's headline in the *Briarwood Times*.

It was comforting to see Tobia waiting for him by the pumpkin cart when Nub arrived back at the farm. No one was home or at the barns, and the truck was gone. He wondered where his parents were, but wherever they were, he knew that when they heard about what had happened at the inn, they would come looking for him at the pumpkin stand.

Loading up the cart with his best pumpkins, Nub said to Tobia, "I saw a monster. You wouldn't believe how horrible that thing was. It looked right at me!" Nub might have had second thoughts about going to the pumpkin stand after his frightening experience, but maybe Nil would come by.

Nub attached the cart to Rudy's harness, and the horse pulled the cart of pumpkins to the main road while Nub and Tobia walked alongside him.

At the stand, Nub's hand-painted sign read: NUB'S PUMP-KINS—SPECIAL HERE!! Nub set up all the pumpkins with their differently carved faces. He and Tobia waited for their first customer, while Rudy picked at grass in the field behind the stand.

Still with the image of the mad monster with the flaming hand fresh in his mind, every once in a while Nub would turn around to look at the edge of the woods beyond the field.

A few cars drove by, but no one stopped. He got a few beeps though, as if to say "Hi, Nub," and he waved back.

Finally, a white station wagon slowed and pulled over. Two little girls climbed out from the back and ran over to the stand; they touched all the pumpkins, trying to decide which one to take home. Then the woman driving the car got out; it was Mrs. Dugan, Nub's teacher and the police chief's wife.

Uh, not really the person I want to see, Nub thought, having left school early—twice. He figured that she already knew that he had been the one who had called the police from the Briarwood Inn.

She put her hand over her heart. "Chester told me about you and Frank Jones! Are you okay? I mean you look okay, but . . ."

"Yeah, I'm fine. The people at the inn aren't, though."

"I know, grey as a catbird, Chester said, and Chef Sprinkle has locked himself in his house and won't come out."

A car pulled up in a hurry and screeched to a halt. From a big grey sedan with smoke coming out of its tailpipe stepped Detective Devlin.

"Uhhh," whispered Nub under his breath. "That guy!" he said louder.

Mrs. Dugan turned and looked.

The pink-faced man in the black hat, suit, and raincoat—only this time with a yellow- and green-striped tie—walked slowly and cumbersomely to the pumpkin stand. He was smoking a big cigar. Tobia's ears pricked backward, and he gave a low growl. Mrs. Dugan busied herself by helping her children decide on two pumpkins.

"I like this smiling one," said the littlest girl.

"Okay, Hazel, that one's for you then." Nub smiled, talking to the little girl and ignoring Devlin.

"And I like this tall one with only one eye," said her bigger sister. The girls giggled.

"Nub, we'll take these two," his teacher said.

"That's four dollars," he said.

"Oh, here's five; keep the change," Mrs. Dugan handed him the money.

"Thanks." Nub took the money and put it in his pocket.

"Beautiful pumpkins, Nub. You have such a knack for growing things, just like your dad."

Nub smiled. "Thanks." At the same time, though, he was very irritated by Devlin's presence.

"Please have your mother write two absent notes, and bring them in on Monday," Mrs. Dugan said.

"Yeah, okay," Nub replied.

Nub couldn't stand that this creep was standing near them, listening. Nub helped carry the pumpkins to the car. Then Mrs. Dugan and her daughters drove off.

Devlin stood looking at all the pumpkins. "Missed school, did ya?" he commented on what he had overheard, but Nub didn't respond.

Nub wished he would leave. He didn't answer anything Devlin asked him. *Ignore him and he'll leave,* Nub thought.

That was the plan, at least. Finally Nub had had enough. "Would you like to buy a pumpkin today or what?"

Devlin's face got a shade pinker. "Nah, got no use for a pumpkin."

Yeah, that's 'cause you have one on your head, Nub thought. *Only it's pink. Must be George Melon's father.* Nub laughed to himself.

"What's so funny?" Devlin asked.

Nub wouldn't reply.

Devlin went on, "I was just out checking the Briarwood Inn, seeing if I could find out anything about what happened there today. I heard about Mr. Jones and some of the guests—"

"I know. I was there. I called the police," Nub interrupted him. "But you know that already deee-tec-tive."

"Ah, yeah. What did ya' see? Some kind of monster, I heard?" Devlin asked. He had his little notepad and pen in his hand.

"Yup, a monster! With a flaming skeleton hand," Nub said bluntly.

"Whoa, come on kid, what did you really see?"

Nub continued, "It ran into the woods behind the inn. Maybe you should go look for it." Nub couldn't help it. This man got under his skin. He really disliked him.

"Yeah, right! Okay, okay, I'll talk to Chief Dugan. I'll have to check on that. Anything else?" He was writing notes in a pad.

"Yeah, you do that," Nub snapped.

A big pumpkin rolled off the table and fell onto the ground, cracking open. "Hey! Gonna put that in your notes?" Nub asked.

Up the gravel road, they heard a horse galloping toward them; coming down from the valley was Jack Turner on Old Tom.

He stopped at the pumpkin stand and jumped off the horse.

"Turner! You're a cowboy, too," called out Devlin. "Got some questions for ya!"

"Not now, Devlin, you best be getting along." Jack Turner stared at him forcefully, as if to say, *I'm not kidding.*

"Well, I guess it can wait." Devlin slipped his notebook in his pocket and walked back to his car.

Jack waited until Devlin started the engine before he spoke. "I saw your note to Nil at the house. I came down the road, looking for her at your farm, but no one was there. I borrowed Old Tom. I was hoping she was here. Have you seen her?" he asked urgently. "I heard what happened at the inn. I can't find her. I think she is in danger."

"From that thing, the monster?" Nub asked.

Jack Turner took a moment to answer. "I hope not."

"Me, too; weird stuff's been happening," Nub was thinking out loud.

"Like what?" Jack Turner quickly responded.

Nub was reluctant to break his promise to Nil about the book or about White Rice, for that matter. But there was the turtle at school—twice. He could mention that. "Well, for one thing, a turtle followed me to school from the river. Now it's hurt, though, or dead, because this miserable kid dropped it on purpose. I don't know if it's okay. . . ."

"Uhhhh," Jack Turner gasped. "Where is the turtle Nub? Can you take me to the turtle?" Jack Turner's tone was urgent.

"Of course I can. It's by the rock at the river under some leaves. At least that's where I left it. Come on. What's wrong?"

Jack Turner answered, "I just need to check the turtle!"

Nub climbed up on Rudy, while Jack Turner rode Old Tom. They galloped up the gravel road into the valley along the Yawning Rabbit River; Tobia ran alongside them.

Taking the horses right to the river, Nub led Jack Turner to the place where he had covered the turtle. It was gone.

"It's not here! It's alive, I guess. It has to be. I put it here."

"Nub, I have to go!" Jack Turner insisted.

"Why? What's wrong?"

"I have to look for Nil at the house! Can you take Old Tom back?"

"Of course, go ahead," Nub answered. "I should go with you, though."

"No, no, but can you come by my house tomorrow morning?" Jack Turner asked. "If I'm there," he added.

"Sure. Why, where else would you be?"

"I must get goin'," was all Jack said, then he hurried down the path toward the stone bridge. "See you tomorrow," he called out.

"Of course, I'll see you tomorrow, first thing," Nub yelled.

When Nub arrived back at the pumpkin stand, his mother and father were waiting for him. Two boys on their bicycles were picking out pumpkins and putting them in their front baskets. They gave Nub's mother the money and pedaled off.

Nub's parents were very relieved to see Nub on Rudy, leading Old Tom. Tobia followed the horses.

Nub slid off Rudy.

Francis Begley put his arm around Nub and hugged him. "Ah, it's good to see you. See, I told you he was all right."

"You weren't here; we were worried about you," Gina Begley hugged her son tight.

"Where were you?" asked Francis. "Why do you have Old Tom?"

"Huh, Jack Turner borrowed him to come see me. He can't find Nil and—"

"Oh, I hope she is okay!" said Gina. "We heard what happened at the inn."

"Hmm, maybe I should go to Jack Turner's," said Francis.

"He asked me to come by in the morning, so I will," Nub told his dad.

"I'll take Old Tom back to the farm and give him a call," Francis Begley said.

"You okay, Mom? You look pale," Nub said, looking at her.

She smiled and nodded. "Yeah, I'm fine 'cause you're fine. Got nervous about you, though. I'll take the car back, Francis," Gina Begley said.

Francis got on Old Tom and went up the road to call Jack Turner. There was no answer at Jack Turner's house, and when Francis Begley went over there before dinner, there was no one home. That night at dinner, Nub told his parents the details about what had happened at the inn and about the monster that he saw.

"I can't believe this was the real problem all along." His father shook his head. "So bizarre. A monster in these times! I don't know, just doesn't sound right to me."

Chapter Sixteen

Turtle News

he next morning was Saturday. Frost glistened everywhere, as if the valley and mountain were sugar coated. Nub did his chores extra early and as fast as he could, then left for Jack Turner's house. He hurried passed the Briarwood Inn. It looked empty and was surrounded by yellow crime-scene tape.

Just past the inn, Nub stepped on something and looked down. It was shiny. He picked it up; it was the string necklace with the key that Nil usually wore around her neck. The string was broken. He hurried to tell Jack Turner.

When Nub arrived at the house, the front door was open. He heard Jack Turner call from upstairs.

"Come on in, Nub!"

Nub went into the foyer as Jack Turner came down the stairs.

Nub held out his hand with the key necklace in it.

Jack Turner's face was serious, and he took the key from Nub.

"She's not here, is she?" Nub asked, feeling a big weight in his heart.

"No, I haven't found her. I was hoping she might have come to see you," Jack said. He tied the broken string together and put it over Nub's head. "You keep this key with you for Nil, okay? That way if Nil finds you first, you will have it for her."

"Okay," Nub agreed.

"Come on in here, Nub." Jack motioned him into the living room.

"Let's talk about the turtle," Jack Turner said. "Can you tell me everything you can remember about the turtle? From the time you first saw it."

"Well, I saw it the other morning for the first time by the river. That was Wednesday. Oh, and it was there again in the afternoon after school. It was eating daisies. Then the next day, it was raining," Nub recalled, "and I saw the turtle at the school by the fence at recess. I brought it back to the river so this foul kid, George, wouldn't bother it. Then on Friday, the turtle showed up at school again. Before I knew it was there, George found it and played catch with it and dropped it on the ground on purpose, hard! It was hurt, and so I took it to the river."

Jack Turner looked terribly distraught by the news.

"I know! I tried to catch the turtle, but I didn't get to it in time," said Nub.

Jack Turner nodded his head as if he understood.

Nub looked around. His gaze fell upon the bookcase, and he saw the green book.

Jack Turner noticed his gaze and looked toward the bookshelf and the green book.

"Nub, there's more, isn't there? You must tell me, son, so I can help Nil and you, too. Things are seriously wrong. I have felt it."

"Nil showed me White Rice and the old green book two days ago," Nub said. "Nil asked me to promise not to say anything, but . . ."

"Did she?" Jack Turner replied.

"Maybe it's the spell of the book that's doing this! Maybe she shouldn't have showed me," Nub added.

"No, no, it's not like that. The spell is to protect the Yawning Rabbit River and the goddess herself," Jack said.

Jack Turner walked to the bookcase and pulled the book from the shelf.

Nub went up to him and looked at the cover of the book; he seemed struck by something. Jack Turner could see in the boy's face that a thought had occurred to him.

Nub touched the symbol and felt the tingle.

"What is it, Nub?"

"Nil said you had the book because it was very special."

"It is."

"This symbol looks like the markings on the turtle's shell," Nub stated.

"Yeah, that's right," Jack Turner confirmed.

"That's strange, right?" Nub asked.

"Well, no, not really . . . actually there is an explanation. It's the symbol of the Great Watcher—and the river goddess, I suppose. It's an old language." The man paused and took a breath. "I'm not Nil's grandfather."

"You're not?"

"No. I'm a friend of the river, so I am a friend of Nil's. I don't know how else to say this to you, so I'll just say it flat out. Nil is the turtle, the turtle is Nil."

"Nil is Daisy?" Nub exclaimed. "We have to find her! *I* have to find her!"

"Yes, we do," Jack Turner, answered. "Nil is the river goddess."

"I thought Violet was the river goddess," Nub said. "Nil told me about her."

"Violet was her mother; she passed over many years ago. Nil is a young river goddess, but she is different from any before her. You see, her father was a mortal man. I'm going to the waterfall at sunset, hoping to find her again. I hope she'll hear the flute." Jack took his flute from his jacket pocket. "This is how I met her in the first place. That's how I got the book. She gave it to me to keep it safe for her."

"I heard you playing the other night," Nub told him.

"That doesn't surprise me," said Jack Turner.

"Okay, I'm coming with you tonight!" Nub declared.

"No, Nub, you have to stay at the farm, in case she comes back to look for you. And furthermore, I want you to keep this book for her. It's got to stay hidden," he insisted.

"Why? What could happen? You mean that monster? You don't think Nil met that thing or that she is dead? Right? River goddesses don't die like that, right?"

Jack Turner shook his head. "Oh, son, no, no; we can't think that way. We have to be strong-minded for Nil. She is very special, very special indeed, and I imagine the monster may know that now, and that is very dangerous for her," Jack Turner said, thinking out loud. "That's my worry."

"What? That monster? What is it?"

"Asheater. Not it—him. You saw him yesterday; that was Ash Miller, one of the Miller twins."

"Do you know him?" asked the boy?

"I saw him a few times when he was a boy, a very troubled boy." Jack Turner stopped speaking, as if he were lost in thought.

"What?" Nub asked. "What?"

The man put his hand on the boy's head affectionately, "Nil found a very good friend in you, didn't she? We're gonna find her, son."

Nub nodded and tried to smile.

Then Jack Turner changed the subject, "You gonna sell your pumpkins today?"

"I was, but . . ."

"No, go do that. Nil might find you. That's my hope. I'll come by as soon as I can. Now, have faith, my boy, in our friend Nil. Be on the lookout."

"Okay," Nub replied.

"Nub, please tell your father thanks for the call and coming by last night. Tell him I'll be in touch real soon if I need his help. For now, let's keep Nil's identity to ourselves, and the Asheater for that matter. You can see how difficult it would be to explain such things. Now, I want you to take the book and hide it where no one else can find it." He handed Nub the book.

"Okay, I can do that," said Nub. He put the book inside his jacket. "I'll keep it safe."

When Nub had closed the door behind him, Jack Turner looked down to the floor. "It's okay; that boy will take very good care of the book. Nil trusted him, and so do I."

Out from under the bookshelf walked Robert Snow, the well-dressed, poetic rat, wearing his coat and the hat with a feather in it. He climbed up a chair, then jumped onto a side table with a lamp. After all these years, he had never been very far away from the little river goddess or the green book; he was a guardian to both. In fact, it was he whom Violet had asked to watch over Nil.

Robert Snow and Jack Turner had been friends for many years, and it was Robert Snow who had alerted Nil that the Millers had the book. The very night the book was first at the Miller's, Nil had snuck in and taken it back. Soon after, the book was given to Jack Turner to keep safe.

After leaving Jack Turner's, Nub stopped by his river rock, but there was no sign of Nil the girl or Nil the turtle. The river and the woods felt eerily quiet.

Where are you, Nil? Nub wondered.

Soon after Nub had put the turtle under the leaves, it had recovered enough to become a girl again. Happy to see White Rice waiting for her in the grass, Nil thought she would go to Jack Turner's house to tell him she was doing okay, then go off to see Nub at his pumpkin stand. She wanted to thank him for what he did for the turtle and possibly explain her identity. Maybe.

On her way to Jack Turner's house, just passed the Briarwood Inn, a dark shadow emerged from the woods onto the path behind her. Before Nil could jump into the river or escape into the woods, Asheater had her in his clutches. He was strong from his most recent attacks on the people at the Briarwood Inn. Nil did not have the strength to break free, but she was able to drop White Rice before Asheater crushed her in Nil's arms.

"Run, White Rice! Go!" Nil told the rabbit, but before the rabbit could move, Asheater kicked it; it flew into the air, then hit the ground.

Nil yelled, "White Rice, get up!"

Asheater motioned to some cave crickets to fetch the rabbit. It would make a good dinner; raw rabbit was one of his favorites. As the cave crickets tried to grab the rabbit, it jumped across the path into the brush. They pounced but discovered that the rabbit had disappeared from under them; luckily, it had found a groundhog's hole and had escaped.

Nil struggled to get away, too. Asheater clutched her neck tightly with one hand, trying to get his flaming skeleton hand close to her head. The fire came close and Nil's hair caught fire. Her long brown hair was in flames. She screamed; in the forest, at that precise moment, the trees shuddered, the birds all flew in the air at once, and small animals—squirrels, raccoons, chipmunks—cowered as if they had been struck. The wind whined a scream of its own, and in the sky, the clouds, for a split second, shattered apart like broken glass. Along with these unnatural phenomena, the river's current stopped.

Nil, barely conscious, opened her eyes; through the torn-open jacket and shirt on Asheater's chest, she saw the arrowhead necklace—the very arrowhead of Angus Gunne's that had killed her father, Daniel Moran. The arrowhead seemed to come alive, something ugly and dangerous reaching for her. Nil cried out, "Help!" And then she collapsed.

Behind Asheater, whose back was to the river, the water churned and swirled. Thousands of droplets rapidly gathered together, and the water elemental appeared, first as a small figure emerging from the surface but quickly growing and towering over them. With its big, river-water fingers, it reached down and put out the fire in Nil's hair. Her burnt scalp steamed. The water elemental bent over Asheater and looked him in the face.

Asheater was completely out of control and ignored him, having forgotten their previous encounter years ago when the fierce water elemental could have been a warning of his dark future. Now Asheater was doing that most forbidden of things: he was hurting the river goddess herself. The great water being bared its big, dog-like teeth and growled.

Oblivious, Asheater raised his flaming hand over Nil's chest, aiming to strike her heart. But before he could, the water elemental lifted Asheater, who still held on to Nil, off the ground and dunked him under the water, holding him under for several minutes. This helped Nil to escape. When the elemental pulled Asheater out of the water, the monster was unconscious; his body hung limp, the flame in his hand was out.

Nil was released into the water and had instinctively become the turtle. She swam to the river bottom for safety. The water elemental tossed Asheater onto the dirt path. He hit the ground with a thump, and it sounded like his bones broke into pieces. The water elemental dissolved back into the river and was gone. Asheater's loyal valley vultures flew overhead, then landed and stood like sentinels by his drenched, motionless body. Clusters of leavils—small, black, leaf-like creatures with eyes and a mouth full of sharp teeth—swirled around him, then covered him like a thick blanket. Cave crickets the size of children poked and pulled him. The crickets began to sting him, and his body jerked.

As if someone had struck a match, a tiny flame reappeared in the skeleton hand; slowly the flame grew larger. Robotically,

Asheater sat up and pushed away the cave crickets. With the leavils still sticking to him, he stood up and looked down into the water. He strained his desperate sunken eyes. His mouth tried to form words. He had not spoken in such a long time he had forgotten how. He struggled to say something. From his throat came a sound; hard to describe, but it was awful and desperate and frightening.

The bruised and burned turtle lay hidden at the muddy bottom of the river. The golden carp swam around the turtle like a watchful nurse or comforting mother.

Above the water's surface loomed Asheater.

This was the first time Asheater had encountered the young river goddess, and vice versa. Asheater sensed that she was different from any of his other victims. Although he hated the river, he realized that she had river magic and a power unlike anyone he had ever attacked, and that interested him. Her extraordinary powers and memories were things he craved. She could be his "cure," her life for his salvation; better yet, she could make him a more powerful man. Asheater didn't know he was a monster—monster's usually don't. He didn't know what he was, who he was, or anything really. He just lived day to day, night by night without purpose or meaning, surviving and existing in a continuous nightmare of cravings.

For all those forgotten years that had passed him by, the boy Ash had lived in an abandoned coal mine, hidden in a remote area of the thick, dark, tangled woods. Little by little, his mind had slipped into a haunted, vicious madness, and he lost any trace of himself as a human. It was he who was responsible for the murders of unfortunate strangers who wandered into "his" woods. Seeming more than just cursed, Asheater barely slept, was tormented by knife-stabbingly painful headaches, and his right hand, once injured by Gunne's arrowhead, burned in constant flames. But the curse "helped," too. It had given him unusual power over creatures such as the cave crickets, ranging in size from as little as a rat to as big as a small man, who stole things for him; the valley vultures, who gathered rotted meat for him to eat; and the wind-traveling leavils, who could go almost anywhere unnoticed. All the creatures spied for him.

Sometime during the middle of the night, Asheater retreated from watching over the river and went into the forest to one of the caves. He would leave the cave crickets to look for the special girl.

Early in the morning, at the bottom of the river, the turtle opened her eyes. Still swimming around her was the carp. The turtle stayed quiet for a few seconds; it seemed as though she were considering the situation. She looked up to the surface; there was no sign of a shadow lurking above the pool. Disobeying orders, the cave crickets had given up.

Inside her shell, the turtle pulled and twisted her body. Pulling hard, she struggled and strained to free her little body from the shell. Nervous by the turtle's actions, the carp swam in fast circles. A cloud of mud stirred up as the turtle struggled with all her strength; eventually, she tore the skin that kept her turtle body attached to the shell. The now "naked," tender, and pale turtle swam away from the empty shell toward some big rocks by the side of the waterfall.

Still submerged in the water, the turtle slowly changed back into a girl. Slipping behind the stream of falling water and up onto a rock, Nil gasped for her breath. She was wearing the same torn, burnt shirt and pants that she had on the day before, and still carried the little bag. Nil put her hand to her head. She had no hair, just a few burnt strands hung limp from her burnt scalp. Nil lay across the rock, trying to recover, taking shallow breaths.

After a while, she lifted herself up and began to climb the side of the waterfall as she had often done. A little way up the steep, rocky face of the cliff, her foot slipped, and she slid back

down into the water. She made a big splash, and she hoped that nothing had heard it. Her body hurt, and her knee was cut from the fall, but she tried to ignore the pain. Nil pulled herself onto the rock again, then slowly and deliberately climbed the waterfall once more. She clicked her tongue to call for White Rice, but there was no sign of the rabbit.

From the pool below, the carp leaped into the air. Nil kept climbing. Panicked, the fish leaped out of the water again and again, trying to call Nil back.

Nil finally reached the top of the waterfall.

Once more, with its last bit of energy, the carp leaped and tried to make it to the top, but it couldn't. Exhausted, it took a few small gasps of breath in the air and muttered her name, "Nil!" Nil heard it, but the fish had hit the water with one final splash.

Nil peered over the ledge. The carp was floating lifelessly on the water's surface. Tears ran down Nil's cheeks, and they fell into the pool below. She lay her head on the ground and sobbed.

Then Nil smelled something sweet in the air. Close by was a hollowed-out log, and growing all around it were yellow rose blossoms, still in bloom even this late in the season. She crawled closer to the flowers. Up through the flowers, a red fox popped out her head.

"Nil! You look awful!" It was Ruby, the fox who frequented the river land.

"Oh, Ruby, I feel awful! I've made a mistake coming here to Briarwood. I must be the most stupid river goddess ever." Nil paused. "I have to leave."

"You can't leave; you're the river goddess," Ruby said.

"I'm only half a river goddess, remember? My father was a mortal," Nil told her. "I should never have been born."

"Nil! What a horrible thing to say," Ruby exclaimed.

Nil looked at the ground, shamefaced; she knew it was a horrible thing to say, really horrible, but she felt really horrible.

"River goddesses don't give up, ever, no matter how difficult life gets," Ruby declared. "You just can't. Look what happened to the carp."

"Oh, that's not my fault," Nil protested, but she knew it was, and she felt terrible about it. "You're a very smart fox. Who are you, anyway, my teacher or something? Are you Mrs. Dugan?" Nil snapped at the fox.

"Who is Mrs. Dugan? Should I know her?" the fox inquired.

"No, you wouldn't know her. I went to school for a little while with other kids, and she was the teacher. A very nice woman, but school didn't work out so well for me."

"I'm sorry about that." The fox meant it.

"Thanks. Well, yeah, school was okay I guess. I liked math a lot . . . and a boy named Nub." Nil smiled for a moment, then went back to her original thought. "Besides, there is no need for a river goddess anymore."

"I don't agree. You can't leave the river, and the river can't leave you," declared Ruby. "And everything beautiful and living depends on the river. You love the river, and the river loves you. It has always been that way."

"Well, I don't know! The river can go where it wants to and so can I. I can go lots of places, maybe where the wild melon heads are from; they have told me about where they live."

"Those ridiculous melon heads! You can't believe what they say, Nil," Ruby insisted.

"Or maybe I'll go hide in the deepest trench in the ocean where the sea dragon-horse lived; the one who came to see my mother!"

"Oh, Nil, don't talk like that," the fox said. "Anyway, what sea dragon-horse?" Ruby inquired, now curious.

Nil realized she had said something that probably no one but she, her mother, and Robert Snow knew about. She changed the subject. "You know, being a river goddess isn't very easy, Ruby. It seems I have made so many mistakes!"

"I know, Nil dear, but you must calm down, please; you're injured. And everyone makes mistakes." Ruby picked some fresh rose blossoms. "Here, eat these, and you'll feel better. They're your favorite."

"No, no, you don't understand!" Nil insisted. Tears were running down her bruised and burnt cheeks again.

"Well tell me then, and I will try," Ruby tried to console the girl. "Tell me about the brave sea dragon-horse that came to see your mother."

Nil took several breaths. "How did you know she was brave?"

"It just sounds brave to me to go to the deepest darkest trench in the ocean. It sounds amazing, really!"

"Well, I guess it couldn't hurt to tell just you about it." Nil sniffed and wiped the tears from her cheeks. "Not too long after my father was killed, the sea dragon-horse visited my mother."

"Why? Did she know your mother?"

"Yes," Nil said, then continued, "The warrior who rode her and fought with her in many battles took sanctuary once in my mother's woods. That was before my father came to the woods. They were hiding from a tyrant emperor's army who wanted them both dead."

"What happened to them?" Ruby asked.

"They stayed for a while with my mother, but when they left, the warrior man was killed and the sea dragon-horse was badly wounded."

"Oh, no!" exclaimed Ruby.

"Yeah, but it was really her heart that was broken. She had loved her warrior; she would have given her life for his and he for hers."

"What was her name, Nil?" Ruby asked.

"I don't know."

"What happened then?"

"After the warrior was killed, the sea dragon-horse left the earthly world and returned to the sea to live in the trench, the deepest place in the ocean that she could find. It was so deep, it was farther down than the highest mountain was tall. Can you believe that?"

"Oh, my! How much more than this waterfall is that?" the fox questioned Nil, pointing at Jumping Grace Falls.

Nil peered over, "Oh, so much more! I don't know."

"Wow," said Ruby. "Then what happened, Nil?"

"The sea dragon-horse stayed in the deep water to be quiet and alone. It *was* pretty quiet, but she found that she was not really alone. Strange little and not-so-little glowing creatures with lights inside them would swim all around her and sometimes tell her things."

Ruby's eyes were fixed on the little river goddess; the story was captivating. Even Nil was forgetting her troubles as she told the fox the legend. Nil ate a rose blossom, then another.

"Like what things? What kind of creatures?" Ruby wanted to know.

"I don't know exactly, ocean creatures that live down there in the deep water. She might have even thought they were angels, the way they were illuminated in the dark water, but they weren't."

"Uh! Maybe they were, "Ruby responded.

"No, they were just sea creatures with special chemicals inside them that lit them up."

"Oh, I see," said Ruby.

"Yeah, well anyway, one day, a very well-informed bright-blue crab said something that reminded the sea dragon-horse of my mother. I forget what it was . . . um, . . . oh yeah! The crab was describing the color of the sky—or maybe it was the color of the water—anyway, the crab said, 'violet blue,' and the sea dragon-horse suddenly silenced the crab. She remembered my mother's name was Violet.

"The great sea dragon-horse had never forgotten my mother's kindness and her beautiful land and river. The sea dragon-horse told the story to the blue crab, then the blue crab told her what had happened to my mother and Daniel. The sea dragon-horse began to cry; her heart was broken once again. She cried and cried, and giant waves were made in the ocean that day, ones that toppled ships and caused tsunamis. The sea dragon-horse, knowing that she would soon die, vowed to go visit the river goddess. She left the deepest trench."

Ruby took a deep breath. "She did?"

"Yes, with her keen senses still intact and with her remaining strength, she left the trench and swam through oceans and rivers, clambered across vast lands and over mountains, and finally reached the Great Ocean that led to the river land. She found my mother with some help from—guess who?"

"Who?" Ruby had to know.

"The little black eyes. It was the only time *ever* that they had given someone the right directions!" Nil continued with her story.

"It was nighttime, and the sea dragon-horse stood before my mother and said, 'I heard of your great loss, and it was my last wish to visit you to tell you how I have never forgotten you and your kindness and your beautiful river land.'

"'Your last wish?' my mother replied, and the sea dragon-horse told my mother the unfortunate news that she was near to death. My mother thanked her for the thoughtful visit, and then told her some happy news: that she was pregnant with Daniel's child, a baby daughter (me, of course), that I would be the very first river goddess/mortal, and that I would take the shape of a turtle rather than a deer."

Nil sighed, remembering that she had left her turtle shell behind for good. She couldn't tell Ruby this; it was too difficult. Nil felt ashamed about what she had done; even worse, she felt that she didn't have courage like the sea dragon-horse, like her mother, or like a river goddess is supposed to.

Nil continued, "Only a few hours later, before the light of dawn, the sea dragon-horse died in front of my mother. Just before she died, she said, 'I swim in your heart, Violet, and in your daughter's heart, too, always. Perhaps you could name her Nil.' My mother agreed that it would be my name."

"Maybe that was her name, too; maybe you are named after her," Ruby said.

"Maybe," answered Nil. "I don't know. Then the sea dragon-horse said to my mother, 'I leave with you a gift for you and for your daughter.' She opened her mouth and out fell one of her big pointed teeth."

Ruby looked at Nil. "That's incredible, Nil! Where is the tooth now?"

"I don't know. I haven't thought of it in a long time, but it must be somewhere—maybe even on the bottom of the river, I guess. I don't think my mother ever gave it to me. What kind of river goddess am I that I don't even know where the sea dragon-horse's tooth is?"

"Don't say that. You are still a young river goddess, Nil," Ruby explained.

The fox and Nil were quiet for a moment.

Nil stood up. "Don't mention a word of this, Ruby, to anyone!"

Ruby nodded. "Okay."

Nil picked a handful of the roses and put them in the little bag around her waist. In it, she carried things such as her favorite colored pebbles, peppermint twigs, acorns, a black-and-white woodpecker's feather, and a red guitar pick that Zachary Lee Bones had given her. Then she walked slowly to the river with Ruby by her side.

Nil dipped her hands into the cool water to wash her face and have a drink. Bending over the water, she saw her reflection, and realized again that most of her hair was gone. She looked up and noticed that the leaves were falling from the trees in unnaturally great numbers and much too fast. She welled up with tears. It seemed as though the trees were crying leaves.

Ruby, too, had tears running down her furry face. Nil bent forward and kissed the fox's wet cheek. "You're a nice fox. The nicest fox I know. Now, don't follow me." Nil turned and began to walk along the river to the north as Ruby silently and sadly watched her.

At that very moment downriver, Nub had found Nil's house-key necklace lying on the path and had gone to see if Nil was at Jack Turner's house.

Chapter Seventeen

I'm No Trash

Jack Turner made his way to the pool below Jumping Grace Falls. He played his flute, hoping that Nil would hear the music and come to the waterfall. He asked the wind to take the melody to her, but the wind seemed disoriented and out of sorts. After playing for about an hour, he saw a swirl in the water. There was something floating there. Putting his flute down on the ground, Jack Turner leaned forward, trying to make out what it was in the last of the evening light.

"Ahhhh!" he cried. It was the dead golden carp. Jack called out, "Nil!" He knew that the carp and Nil were tied in spirit to the river. This was a dreadful sign. He dove into the water and grasped the carp. He swam down to the muddy rocky bottom, feeling around with his other hand, just missing the empty turtle shell in the grasses next to a river rock. Jack Turner was relieved not to find Nil lying at the bottom. When he surfaced, he was still holding the dead carp. He swam to the side of the pool and was ready to climb out when he saw someone was standing there. Looking up, he could see the face of Devlin, who was holding a thick piece of wood in one hand.

"Uhhhh, Devlin, what the devil are you doing here?"

"Where is it, Turner?" Devlin demanded, pushing Jack back down into the water.

Jack Turner resurfaced. "Where's what, you fool?"

Devlin swiped at Jack's head with the big piece of wood and hit him. "You know what. The book, where is it?"

Devlin caught hold of Jack Turner's coat and pulled him onto the ground. "Stand up, Turner!"

Jack Turner, still holding the carp, got to his feet. "This is what your investigation is about? Uhhhh, you have no idea what your dealing with. Let me give some advice, leave this place while you can!"

"It's mine! It was mine years ago when Harold Miller was gonna sell it to me for next to nothin'. That idiot didn't know what I know. That's no ordinary book!"

"No, it's not, and it's never going to be *yours*—never! It's impossible. Get out of here now, Devlin. I have more important things to worry about than you, you lowlife."

"You don't need to worry about me, Turner. That book is gonna make me rich! Tell me, where is it? Finally, I'm gonna be rich. Gonna make Mike Crawley important, you hear. Now get it for me!"

"Who is Mike Crawley? Is that you? You're not even Devlin? I knew you were a swindler and cared nothing for the people of Briarwood!" Jack Turner smacked Devlin in the face with the carp.

Devlin struck back, hitting Jack hard on his head with the piece of wood. Jack Turner struggled to stay standing, but his legs gave out, and he collapsed, falling backward. His head was bleeding. Before he fell back into the water, Devlin caught him by the arm.

"I'm not kidding, Turner, I'll kill you if I have to!"

Jack Turner tried to focus his eyes on the man, but his vision was blurry and his head was spinning.

From the woods behind Devlin leaves crunched; someone or something was approaching. Devlin let go of Jack Turner's arm, and Jack fell back into the water with a splash. Devlin ran off down the path toward Briarwood, and three cave crickets arrived at the scene. They fished Jack Turner out of the water and pulled him onto the ground; in his hand, he still held on to the carp. A cave cricket yanked it up in a hurry and bit off its head. The others tried to grab the headless fish, but the first cave cricket gulped the rest of the fish down, gnashing its teeth. From the top of the waterfall, Ruby the fox peered over. Quietly, she inched her way down the steep path. She followed the cave crickets, who were dragging Jack Tuner into the woods.

The next morning, eerie and ominous clouds formed in the sky over the river; they looked like a long ribbon. News of more attacks by Asheater spread quickly in Briarwood. Looking overhead, the people cowered and ran into their houses; giant valley vultures circled high in the sky over the town, casting big, dark shadows and watching the people's every move. In the backstreets and alleyways, cave crickets darted, sneaking through basement windows. Leavils floated in the windless air, biting and stinging like mosquitoes whenever they landed on bare skin.

To make matters even worse, in the window of Joe's coffee shop hung a sign: NO NO-UMBRELLA PEOPLE. By the end

of that day, other stores had hung up similar signs. An ugly tension was building; the umbrella people and the no-umbrella people began to argue, and fights broke out.

That same day, the Briarwood School closed down, and the train made its final stop at Briarwood station; from then on, the train just whizzed by without stopping. No one wanted to risk meeting the monster.

Nub waited all that day and night, hoping that Nil would come by or he would hear from Jack Turner, but neither happened. When he called the house, no one answered the phone, even though he tried several times.

Nub decided he had to go to Jack Turner's house, regardless of the fact that his parents had said to stay on the farm. He left the green book carefully hidden under a loose plank in the barn floor under the hay in Sienna's stall. Tobia wouldn't let anyone strange near the barn, and Sienna wouldn't let any stranger in her stall. With that kind of double security system, even the author, Robert Snow, would have agreed it was a good place.

When Nub arrived at Jack Turner's house, the door was open, the lock broken. Nub called out from the entrance, "Jack Turner! Nil!" No one answered.

He walked into the living room. Most of the books were off the shelves and thrown across the floor. The chair was over turned. He started to check upstairs when he heard, "No one is upstairs either," coming from under the bookcase.

Nub saw "something" move under the bookcase. He thought his eyes were playing tricks on him. He got down on his knees and looked under the bottom shelf. He saw a silver-grey rat, wearing a black coat and a very fancy hat. They just looked at each other for a moment.

"Hello, I'm Robert Snow," said the rat.

"The author Robert Snow?" Nub had not imagined that he could have been a rat.

"Yes," answered the rat.

"I'm Nub."

"I know, and you have the book. Is it safe?"

"Yes, it is. I'm looking for Jack Turner. Have you seen him? Or Nil!"

"No, I'm afraid not," the rat answered and came out from under the bookshelf.

"I haven't seen Jack Turner since yesterday. Someone was in here looking for the book, though. I only saw the shoes, but whoever it was smelled like cigars."

Nub's eyes grew wide, "Uhh, Devlin!"

"Yes, well, that book is nothing to mess with, I can tell you that. Jack Turner left yesterday and has not returned. I had hoped you were him."

"I am worried about Jack Turner and Nil. I'm gonna go look for them."

"I'm going with you then."

"Okay," Nub agreed. "Come on."

Nub and Robert Snow went out onto the front porch.

"May I?" Robert Snow was pointing to Nub's backpack.

"Yes, please. Come on."

Nub put his red backpack down on the floor, and Robert Snow climbed onto it, holding on to the straps.

On their way back to the farm, while passing the Briarwood Inn, Nub noticed the yellow police tape had fallen down across the top of the stairs on the porch. He saw something moving past the windows. "Did you see that, Robert? Someone's in there!" The boy hurried to the end of the property and climbed up the hill along the hedges. He made his way to the side of the inn. He heard something or someone moving around. He went to a window, but he couldn't see in.

"Robert," Nub whispered.

"Yes?"

"Climb on my head and see if you can see in the window."

Robert scurried up Nub's neck and onto the top of his head and looked in the window. "Yes, I see someone! There's a man. His back is to me."

"What's he doing?"

"Um, he's looking at the books on the shelf. Uh!"

"Devlin!" they said in unison.

Just then Nub stepped on a stick, which cracked under his boot. Nub crouched down below the windowsill. He could hear footsteps walking over to the window.

The boy and the rat stayed perfectly still and held their breath, waiting until they heard the footsteps move away. Robert dashed down Nub's head and into the pack. The boy hurried toward the hedges and ran for the stone bridge. At the bridge Nub stopped. Robert Snow climbed onto his shoulder.

"Devlin's no detective. He's a lying thief!" Nub said.

"He's not a noble thief, either, I can tell you that. I knew a noble thief once," the rat said. "They named the river after him! That's how noble he was."

Nub realized that the rat was talking about Sean the rabbit thief.

Swiftly, Nub headed back to the farm. Once there, he retrieved the book from the barn floor. He checked the house to be sure it was empty, then he took the book into the living room and sat down. Tobia lay at Nub's feet, while Robert Snow stood on the top of the chair, looking over the boy's shoulder.

Suddenly, they heard something rustling at the front door. Tobia growled. Nub hid the book under the chair and went to the window. He looked out, and his eyes grew wide. "Look, it's White Rice!"

Nub opened the door. The white rabbit with the tan patch around its eye was covered in dirt and soot; it stood there trembling.

A large shadow loomed overhead. Nub looked up just as a valley vulture swooped down to grab the rabbit, but Nub beat him to it. Nub clutched the rabbit in his hands and slammed the door shut.

Bam! The vulture hit the door hard and squawked loudly, as if to say, "Let me in!" For a while, it stood outside the door. Nub, still holding the rabbit, watched it from the window. Finally, it flew away to report to Asheater the whereabouts of the little river goddess's rabbit, hoping that maybe the goddess herself would be close by. Nub and Robert worried that some-one—or some*thing*—else might come along soon.

"Listen, Robert, its dangerous for everyone—my parents included—to keep White Rice here," Nub said, putting the rabbit down on the floor near the warmth of the fire.

Robert Snow ran down the arm of the chair and jumped onto the floor. He went over to the rabbit. Tobia sniffed White Rice and nudged her with his nose.

"Where's Nil then?" questioned Robert.

Nub carefully opened the door and looked around. He called her name, just in case.

There was no response.

"It's amazing that the rabbit found you all by itself," Robert declared.

Nub picked up White Rice and went into the kitchen. He got a rag and cleaned and dried her. He set her down on the floor near Tobia's bowl of water; she drank a few little sips. He broke off some small pieces of carrot and put them next to the bowl. She nibbled at them while Nub, Tobia, and Robert stood there watching.

"I'm going to look for Nil. I gotta do something! I just can't stay here and do nothing! I'll go back to Jack Turner's house, then take it from there," Nub told the rat.

"This is extraordinary. Yes, we must go," the rat agreed. "Of course, Nub, I am coming with you."

"Okay," Nub agreed. "I've got to go now before my parents come home, or they'll never let me leave." Nub flew up the stairs, three steps at time, to grab a sweater and a rain jacket from his bedroom. He hurried into the kitchen and looked around. He wasn't planning to be gone long but better safe than sorry. These days, you could never know what might happen. He took a flashlight, matches, a candle, and filled a water bottle. He also grabbed a few pieces of bread, a chunk of cheese, apples, three carrots, and four pieces of apple cake. "I'm taking cheese for you, Robert," he called out from the kitchen, "and carrots for White Rice."

"Oh, thank you. Might you have honey cakes?" the rat asked, thinking back to Finn's honey cakes in Sean's bag.

"No, but I've got apple cake," said Nub.

"Excellent!"

Back in the living room, Nub placed the rabbit in his now full backpack. "Just for now, White Rice; we're in a hurry." Nub lowered his opened hand to the floor. "Come on!" he said to the rat.

Robert Snow buttoned his jacket and fixed his hat with the feather more firmly on his head, then he hopped into Nub's hand. Nub placed him on top of the backpack where he could find a good strap to hold on to. Tobia lifted his head and looked at Nub.

"You stay here, Tobia. I won't be long. You watch the farm."

Tobia lay his ears flat against his head and sighed.

Nub scribbled a fast note and put it on the table in the kitchen. It read: *Dear Mom and Dad. Be right back! Just needed to check on something very important! Please be careful! Love, Nub.*

He knew that they would worry and be upset with him, but what could he do; he had to go. He moved fast, so it wouldn't take that long—maybe.

He was almost out the back door when he stopped. "I shouldn't leave the book, even for just a little while."

"Probably not," said Robert Snow.

Nub hurried back into the living room and retrieved the book from under the chair. His fingers tingled as he put it in the backpack next to White Rice, who was now sleeping, and closed the flap. "I won't let anything happen to them," the rat assured Nub from his position atop the pack.

Nub hurried down the path past the empty Briarwood Inn. As he approached the front porch of Jack Turner's house, he stopped and caught his breath. There was no sign that anyone had been there since he had left. He stood on the porch, thinking.

"We still have a little bit of light left, and I gotta check one place before it gets dark: the waterfall," Nub said. "Then we'll go back to the farm, I guess." Nub was disappointed not to have found any clues yet.

The rat nodded.

With every step, Nub tried to be quiet, but this was such a difficult time of the year to try to do that; crunchy leaves were everywhere.

They could hear the sound of the waterfall, but it didn't seem as loud as usual; it was dwindling. By the edge of the diminishing pool below the waterfall, Nub spied something silver lying on the ground. He picked it up. It was Jack Turner's flute.

He called out, "Jack Turner!" Nothing. "Nil!" Still nothing. "Maybe I should play it," Nub said.

Robert vigorously nodded. "Yes, yes, try anything!"

Nub put the flute to his mouth and blew a simple sound. He did it again, then listened. It was gradually getting darker; the leaves were rapidly falling off the trees. The silence was heavy. Again, Nub played a note on the flute, then stopped.

"I'm not going back to the farm. I can't," Nub said.

The rat adjusted his hat, something he did when he was thinking. "I'm with you."

Nub kept the flute and headed down the dark path alongside the waterfall. After a while, he stopped. The path now seemed more like a narrow footpath or a deer track, and the sound of the waterfall was fainter.

"I'm not sure which path this is. I don't hear the waterfall so much," he told Robert Snow.

The rat didn't answer.

"Robert! You there?"

"Yes! Yes, I'm here," whispered Robert. "I hear something."

"What?" Nub listened. He heard it now, too, rustling footsteps. They were moving closer.

"You think it's Jack Turner?" Nub said quietly. His heart started to pound. He began to imagine the monster man he had seen the other day.

From the bushes, something big bumped into Nub and knocked him over. Nub fell down hard on the path and dropped the flashlight and the flute. The pack was mostly knocked off his shoulders. Robert Snow tumbled off into the grass. The backpack flap opened and out hopped White Rice onto the grass as well.

"It's you, pumpkin kid," said a familiar gruff, slurred voice. "I heard ya' tawkin' to sssssomeone. Who waaasss it?" Devlin shoved him. "What are ya' doin' here? Who were you talkin' to?" he demanded, yanking Nub up by his clothes. He smelled like alcohol.

Devlin picked up the flashlight. Nub picked up the backpack quickly, before Devlin could. It was lighter. No rabbit and no rat. Was the book in there? He couldn't look now, that was for sure.

Devlin shoved him again. "Who were you talking to?"

"Myself," Nub answered. Nub's mouth was bleeding, and he wiped it with his sleeve.

"What are you doing out here kid? You some kind of boy scout or something?" Devlin laughed. "Tryin' to earn your monster badge!" He laughed again. "Aren't ya' scared of monsters, kid?"

"Leave me alone," Nub told him. "The only monster I see is you!"

"I asked you what you were doin' here."

"I was looking for Jack Turner and Nil, but I'm goin' home now." Nub turned and started to head down the path.

"What do you take me for, a fool?" Devlin snarled, grabbing the backpack and yanking Nub backward.

"No, a drunk liar," answered Nub.

"A liar with a knife!" Devlin yanked on him. It was then that Nub saw Devlin had one of Chef Sprinkle's big butcher's knives, and he was waving it in the air.

"Come on, boy hero, this way! Head up there." Devlin pointed the flashlight beam onto the path and poked Nub in the back with the point of the knife.

Nub was thinking about his options, about maybe making a run for it, but Devlin had a firm hold of his backpack, and Nub wouldn't slip it off, even to escape. The green book was in it, and Nub knew that Devlin wanted it. Nub couldn't let him get it.

They came to a clearing at the edge of the old abandoned Miller property. Devlin flashed the light onto the big, strange statues, now covered with ivy and standing in high grasses.

"We're goin' in the house. Keep walkin'." Devlin flashed the light across the property onto the door of the front porch. They got to the front steps, and Nub went up the stairs.

"Open the door," Devlin said.

Nub tried the doorknob. "It's unlocked!" Nub said, surprised.

"Just go in!" Devlin pushed him at the door.

Nub went into the large entrance hall. On all the walls were portraits of the Millers and other strange pictures they had collected. Devlin flashed his light on the walls.

"Uh, the Miller's twins," Nub said. "Which one is Ash, I wonder?"

"Who cares about those brats." Devlin swept the light around the room.

"What's that smell? Like a nasty swamp. Ugh!" Nub gagged.

"Yeah, smelled it the other day. Look here." Devlin shone the flashlight onto the walls covered with thick, black mold. "Could have sworn the walls were talkin', too."

"Maybe it's haunted," Nub said.

"Yeah. Something's here! Gonna getcha, too," Devlin mocked him.

However, the truth was that Devlin had been there earlier that day, and the sounds coming from the walls had scared him away before he could look around much. Now the coward was back with Nub. They walked into the big library. The shelves were mostly empty, and the floor was covered with books; proof that Devlin had at least gotten that far in his search.

"You ever been here before, in this house?" Devlin asked.

"Nope," Nub said.

"Go that way." Devlin pushed Nub toward the kitchen, still holding onto his jacket. "Haven't been in there yet."

Nub walked down the long hallway into the kitchen. Big pots still hung from the ceiling like large bats.

Devlin shined his light on all the walls; against the one wall, a big wooden cupboard had collapsed in pieces and lay on the floor in a heap with broken dishes and bowls around and under it. Behind it, half a door was showing in the torchlight.

"Hey, look at that! Clear that stuff away, and let's take a look behind that door," Devlin commanded Nub. "I think we may have found something."

Nub cleared away the debris and pushed at the remains of the cupboard with his body to reveal the entire door.

"Open it," said Devlin.

Nub pulled the door. It was very tight, but Nub got it open.

Devlin shined the light down the stairs and the long dark hallway.

"Ah! We got something now! I can feel it in my soon-to-be-rich bones. Go boy!"

Nub went down the stairs. The hallway had passages leading off it to different storerooms: some rooms held old jars of food and boxes, others had all kinds of lamps, dining room chairs, and other junk.

"Ah, where is it, where is it? Gotta find it," Devlin was mumbling to himself.

At the end of the main hallway was a small, round, metal door, "Looks like on a submarine," Nub said.

"Who cares what it looks like, open it!" Devlin shouted at Nub.

Nub opened the door. Its rusty hinges squeaked. Devlin shone the flashlight down so that Nub could see the bottom some twenty feet below.

Nub leaned in and looked down; the floor was cluttered with junk. "Oh, just trash is in here," Nub told him.

While Nub was leaning over the opening, Devlin took the opportunity to look into Nub's backpack. Nub tried to stop him, but he was kind of stuck in the round opening. Devlin caught sight of the green book and grabbed it out of the pack.

"This is it! At last, my great fortune! Now get lost kid!" Devlin pushed Nub and his pack through the hatch, and Nub fell down into the room with the trash. He hit the floor with a thud.

He heard Devlin yelling from above. "Ah! Finally! Thank you, no-umbrella brat! You've made me a rich and happy man!"

Nub's head hurt and he was a little dizzy, but he made himself get up. The book was gone. He had to get out of here to go after Devlin. He'd lost his backpack during the fall, so he felt around on the floor for it. When he found it, he reached in for his flashlight, but then he remembered that Devlin had it. Oh, but he had packed a candle and a full box of matches! Good. Feeling around in the bag, he found them. He struck a match, then lit the candle. The pitch black turned to a glow. Nub thought he heard paper rustling and moved the candle toward the sound. He saw a lump under a worn purplish blanket; it looked like something was there. Nub pulled off the dusty blanket. Through the film of swirling dust he saw a figure.

"Uhhhhhh!" Nub gasped. He was looking at a strange boy with a big coin for a head.

Penny Boy's eyes grew wide. He lifted something up to Nub, as if he were trying to give him something. Nub stared back at the coin-headed boy, then looked at what he was holding. It was a box.

Nub shook his head "no," then asked, "What . . . who are you? What are . . . ?"

The dust-covered Penny Boy held out the equally dusty metal box again.

Again Nub shook his head. "No. What is that? I don't want it. Who are you?"

Penny Boy took a small piece of paper and wrote on it, then showed it to Nub.

Nub held the candle to the paper and read it out loud: "I'm no trash."

"Okay, okay," he said. "Of course not. Have you been here in this room for . . . ?" Nub asked in disbelief but couldn't even finish the question.

The coin-headed boy didn't do anything.

"Who are you?"

Penny Boy wrote again. Nub read it: "Penny Boy."

Then he wrote more. "I wait for Dusty." Penny Boy pointed at Nub and stood up.

"What? Oh, no, no . . . um, let's see . . . uh . . ." Nub realized that this boy couldn't answer his questions if he had no mouth.

Penny Boy showed him the note again.

"I wait for Dusty," Nub read out loud. *Oh no, he thinks I'm Dusty!*

"I'm Nub," he said. *And now's probably not the time to tell him that Dusty was murdered by his own brother,* he told himself. "We gotta get out of here, right now," he told Penny Boy.

Using the blanket, Nub brushed off the dust that covered Penny Boy's coin head, while the boy cast him puzzled looks and studied his face.

"Come on, let's get out of here," Nub said. "I'll explain what's going on later. Let me think now. How are we gonna do this?"

Penny Boy touched Nub's shoulder, then pointed to Nub's shoes.

"Yeah, that would be great. I'll step on your shoulders and climb out, then use this blanket to pull you out. Don't worry; I work on a farm, so I'm strong." Nub smiled.

Nub used the candle to look at all the things on the floor. "Hey, I have this," Nub said, holding up a book: *The Adventures* of *Kurt Burning Trail.* "We'll have to leave this stuff for now, though; we can come back for it."

Penny Boy held the metal box close to his chest, refusing to let it go.

"We gotta travel light right now, okay?" Nub tired to coax him, but Penny Boy would not part with the metal box of seeds. He had kept them safe all this time.

"Okay, you can bring it," said Nub, seeing how important it was to him. "Here, I'll put that in my backpack. It will be okay."

Penny Boy gave the metal box to Nub, who put it in the pack. Nub buckled it up and put it on his shoulders. "Okay, Penny Boy, I gotta blow out this candle. We will be doing this in the dark, but we need to save the candle." Nub blew it out and stuck it in his back pants pocket; the matches went into a front pocket. In the dark, he called to Penny Boy, "Okay, come here and stand still."

Penny Boy moved over to the wall below the round, metal door, and Nub pushed down on the boys shoulders to get him to crouch. Taking the blanket, Nub stepped carefully on Penny Boy's shoulders, then Penny Boy stood up, straight and strong—which was remarkable considering that he been locked up for all these years.

Nub stretched to reach the edge of the round door, but he couldn't quite get there. He placed one foot on top of Penny Boy's coin head, then the other. Now he could reach easily. "Perfect, Penny Boy, perfect!"

Once he had hold of the edge, he pulled himself up. In no time, Nub was through the door. He took out the candle and lit it, then placed it on the floor by the door. He lowered the blanket. "Grab it, Penny Boy!" Penny Boy looked up and reached for the blanket.

Nub pulled Penny Boy to the opening. His coin head bumped the side of the door, making a loud clanking sound.

"Oh, sorry," Nub apologized, but Penny Boy seemed not to be bothered.

Nub pulled the boy through onto the hallway floor. At last, after twenty years, Penny Boy was free.

They hurried up the hallway to the stairs that led to the kitchen, then walked under the big hanging pots into the entrance hall and toward the open front door. Penny Boy stopped. Nub turned to see what he was doing. "Come on, we gotta go now. I have to get the book back."

Penny Boy looked at the portraits of the Miller's in the candlelight. He pointed to the picture of Dusty and Ash and looked at Nub.

Nub nodded "yes" as if he understood, but he was in a hurry. Suddenly, they both heard it: a wet, gushy, moving sound; a kind of syrupy humming. Then snarling, hissing, growling, and moaning noises came from behind the black, mold-covered walls.

"We should get out of here now, Penny Boy," Nub insisted, but Penny Boy walked closer to the walls where the thickest black mold was, and the sounds seemed louder! All around them, the walls seemed to bend like soft putty being pushed from the other side.

"This house is haunted, right?" Nub brought the candle closer to the wall. All around them, thousands of parasitic, soul-sucking worms fell like wet tangled string from the walls, but it continued moving and twisting and writhing on the floor. "Ugh, that's disgusting," exclaimed Nub.

The soul crawlers stuck their ugly heads out of the walls; they had pointed, cracked teeth and were covered in worms that were dropping to the floor. Then the heads dropped to the floor, with thumps, and moved all around, rolling and creeping, making biting sounds.

"Ahhhh!" Nub backed away from them, almost falling. Instead of backing away, Penny Boy just stood there and looked one of the creatures right in the eyes.

"What are those things? What is that? This place is crawling with them!" Nub exclaimed. "Penny Boy, don't get any closer!"

Penny Boy was now so close, it seemed to be a deadly stupid thing to do, but the creature froze under Penny Boy's gaze; it could only moan and hiss. As if Penny Boy's gaze were the right combination to a safe, the creature opened its mouth wider and wider, revealing a mouth full of broken sharp teeth. More wriggling worms dropped to floor from the soul crawler's face, and the more that dropped to the floor, the more that came out of the face, out of its mouth and eye sockets—until there were hundreds of them.

"Whoa, Penny Boy, let's go," Nub insisted.

Penny Boy didn't listen. Instead, without hesitation, he reached deeply into the soul crawler's open mouth, as if he were feeling around for something.

"It's gonna bite your hand off!" Nub warned him.

Reaching even deeper into the head, Penny Boy finally found what he was looking for. He pulled his hand out. He backed away from the wall. The walls were suddenly quiet, and the air felt immediately fresher.

Nub looked at the wall. The soul crawler's face was frozen like a plaster statue; the worms dried up and fell to the floor like ashes. All the other soul crawlers rolling on the floor or poking out of the walls fell dead to the ground, dried up like old leaves.

Penny Boy opened his hand to show Nub what he had retrieved from the head of the hideous creature.

"What is that?"

Penny Boy was holding a smooth blue stone. It glowed in his hand. He had retrieved a soul stone, something like a powerful, life-giving battery, but he couldn't explain that to Nub. Instead, Penny Boy just put the stone in his pocket.

"You're amazing," Nub said. "And fearless! Okay, we've really gotta go now." Nub blew out the candle and stuck it back in his pocket.

Nub looked at the coin-headed boy as they walked outdoors. He was sorry that he had never come here before. *Maybe I would have found him years ago*, Nub lamented.

Penny Boy went over to an old, broken-down greenhouse. He just stood there, looking at the broken pots and dead plants, perhaps trying to make sense of what had transpired. Then Penny Boy hurried toward the woods on the deer path that Nub had traveled on earlier. It seemed that Penny Boy had seen enough and had made up his mind about something.

"Wait, Penny Boy! Where you going?" But Nub knew, he was looking for Dusty, who was still very much alive to Penny Boy.

Penny Boy went down the path. Nub followed. They were headed for the waterfall.

"Penny Boy," Nub called. "Do you know Robert Snow?"

Penny Boy stopped and turned around; he shook his head no.

"How about a girl named Nil?"

Penny Boy shook his head no again.

"How about Jack Turner? He's a man who plays a flute, a pennywhistle."

Penny Boy shook his head no a third time.

"Well, I have to find them and the green book."

Penny Boy looked at Nub. Nub had at last mentioned something he knew about.

"What? You've seen the green book?"

Penny Boy nodded.

Nub thought of the spell the book could cast. Maybe that's how Penny Boy got that coin head. It could be a curse, but he didn't think so. No, there must be another explanation as to who Penny Boy was and where he came from, but for now that mystery would have to wait.

Looking at the coin-headed boy, Nub said, "I think I should take you home to the farm."

But Penny Boy had his own plan: find Dusty.

Chapter Eighteen

A Page Is Turned

Penny Boy came to a familiar place and knelt down. It was the old hollowed-out log where he had once spilled the rose seeds and found the green book, but Nub didn't know that. Penny Boy looked at the few roses still in bloom that had grown from the seeds and spread over the years. Penny Boy sat down on the log.

"Okay, good idea; break time." Nub sat down on the log and opened his pack. He took an apple from his bag and offered Penny Boy one, but Penny Boy had no mouth. Nub had taken a couple of bites when he heard something; so did Penny Boy.

A sudden breeze blew by them. *Maybe finally we'll have some rain*, Nub thought, looking up at the bulky, immovable clouds. "Maybe a storm is coming through and will blow these weird clouds away. You know, Penny Boy? That would be good. You see, the river is disappearing into the sky." He pointed at the clouds. "Can you tell?" he asked.

A strong gust of wind blew, and a piece of paper came flying through the air and landed near Nub's feet. Nub snatched it up. To his amazement it was Sean's map from the green book!

"Oh! This is amazing! Look. Sean's map from the green book." He showed Penny Boy. Nub looked around them and behind them.

They heard the screaming groan of a man and thunderous, heavy footsteps nearby in the woods.

"Come on!" With the map in his hand, Nub grabbed his backpack and stood up. He pulled Penny Boy off the log and hid behind a thick cluster of holly bushes. Nub quickly put the map in his pack.

When he looked up, he saw Devlin coming up the path to the hollowed-out log with the green book in his hand. Devlin was trembling and walking with jerky movements. His shirt was ripped open. Pages flew out of the book and swirled around him in the air.

He was fighting with the pages, swatting them with one hand as if he were being attacked by bees, stung by each letter

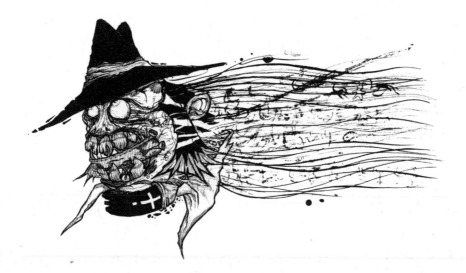

Nub and Nil and the Yawning Rabbit River   219

and each word. Everywhere the pages touched him, words were being written on his skin, as if he were being tattooed. The symbol on the cover of the book seemed to come alive, rising from the book and becoming larger in size, turning in slow circles. It was three-dimensional.

Frightened, Devlin's head spun in circles, watching the symbol turn faster and faster. The wind stirred up again in force. More pages from the book flew out one by one and swirled in a whirlwind. Devlin screamed again and tried to throw the book on the ground, but it seemed fixed to his hand. "No, no!" he screamed. "Let me go!" He covered one ear as if a noise of some kind were hurting him.

Then the spinning symbol exploded and disappeared; the cover of the book was torn open like a wound. The pages ripped themselves out of the book more rapidly and seemed to be attacking Devlin, slicing him, making paper cut after paper cut. The words from the pages were now a foreign language of symbols and images and voices, imprinting themselves onto the man's skin.

Suddenly, Devlin began to change. His black pants stuck to his legs, and within seconds, his legs had transformed into an animal's legs, with cloven hoofs and metal screws through the ankles. Devlin tried to run, but he couldn't. He screamed for help, but nothing could help him now. The spell of the book was taking him. Each page, like his personality, was splitting apart; like a book is divided into chapters, he was no longer a person. His face changed as his skin was torn off. His mouth, much larger now that his lips were missing, showed only his teeth.

Then a metal plate covered Devlin's mouth, which was bolted in place with screws and little iron nails. The screws squeaked and scraped as they tightened. Devlin could not speak with his locked mouth, but some voice was talking—it was his new master. Mike Crawley, who had posed as Detective Devlin, was now the cursed Mr. Page, more like a cumbersome beast than a man. His almost useless arms were chained, allowing them very little movement. If only he had heeded Jack Turner's warning not to mess with the book.

"Look around, Mr. Page! It must be somewhere," the master's voice said. "Find it, Mr. Page." The voice was coming from the man's skin!

Mr. Page gawked at the ground, stepping clumsily on some of the roses and crushing them. He tripped over the log and fell, and he whined. When he got up, which was slowly, he was disoriented and woozy.

"Look, Mr. Page, you must find it."

Mr. Page pounded his skin, trying to make the voice shut up. He was moving closer to the holly bushes when from behind him, a cave cricket jumped on his back. More cave crickets came up from behind, startling him. He ran away into the woods, much to the disapproval of the voice, who commanded him: "Stop, Mr. Page!" But Mr. Page didn't stop, and the cave crickets chased him into the forest.

Nub looked at Penny Boy. "Shhhhh, wait here. I'm gonna look around." Nub carefully and quietly went to the hollowed-out log and looked around on the ground and in the rose bushes. There, under some leaves, lay a giant, triangular, pointed tooth. It was at least three inches long. Nub couldn't have known that he had found the tooth of the warrior sea dragon-horse. All along, the charm had been carefully hidden behind the symbol of the Great Watcher inside the cover of the green book; the tooth was the reason the book held a spell, if taken, and why Nub felt the buzz when he touched the book. Nub picked up the tooth.

He quickly returned to Penny Boy. "What kind of tooth do you think this is?" he asked Penny Boy, forgetting he couldn't speak. So he answered the question himself, "I don't know, maybe a great white shark!"

Penny Boy nodded his head in agreement. It seemed like a good guess. Nub put the tooth in his pants pocket.

Just then, four huge valley vultures flew overhead and landed by the pool at the bottom of the waterfall. They peered down into the water. Nub and Penny Boy peered over the top of the falls to watch them.

Nub sat back and took out the map. The moon was only a week since being full and still bright enough to see by. Nub studied the map. He tapped Penny Boy on the back, and the boy turned around.

"New plan, Penny Boy," Nub whispered. "I have Sean's map and this tooth." He took the tooth out of his pocket and held it up. "We're going that way." Nub pointed north, the opposite direction of Briarwood and toward the Great Forest.

Penny Boy nodded, and that was it.

"Okay," Nub said. "I'm leaving a sign here for Nil, Robert Snow, or Jack Turner; they'll know what it is." He kneeled down and with the tooth, he drew the symbol of the Great Watcher and an arrow pointing the way they would be traveling.

"Okay, we can go." Off they went, following in Nil's footsteps—only they didn't know that.

Chapter Nineteen

Explain Such Things

It was a long two days ago when Nil, wounded and not feeling well, slowly walked away from Ruby, the fox, at the top of the waterfall and into the Great Forest. At one point, she had come across a low stone-wall circle in the center of the forest.

This was written about in the second half of the green book; it was the very place where the animals had the meeting the night Sean the rabbit thief promised to find her mother Violet and win the river.

Sitting down on one of the stones, Nil thought, *No river goddess ever felt like this. I should have been something with wings, not a turtle, so I could fly away.* Then she remembered that she wasn't even a turtle anymore.

Her hand touched something wet and gushy. "Uhh!" she jumped up and stepped on something. "Squish!" She lifted up her foot to look at the bottom of her shoe. Whatever it was, it was smooshed and bloody. *What kind of bug was that?* She took another step and squished another one and then another one. *What are they?* She bent down to look closer and could not believe what she saw; they were eyeballs on the ground.

She quickly looked around. Then she saw a figure, crouching and hiding behind one of the stones. "Who are you?" she called to it, but there was no answer. "Are you the Great Watcher?" *What with so many eyes,* she thought.

She walked around the other side of the wall to the stone. "Ahhh!" Nil gasped.

It was a two-legged figure with grayish lumpy arms and big hands with large broken nails. Its head was covered with dripping goo, and eyes continuously dropped down from its face and fell onto the ground, making puddles of goo and eyeballs.

The thing cowered and turned away, knowing it was hideous. It had come to this place to hide away forever, never thinking anyone, especially a little river goddess, would discover it.

Nil found herself standing in the goo puddle, and her feet were soaked with it. "How long have you lived here?" she asked, but it didn't answer. "You're not the Great Watcher, are you?"

Nil sat down again on the stone wall some distance from the gooey, eye-dripping creature and looked at it. "Isn't that tiring, having all that dripping from you all the time?" She expected it to smell foul, but it didn't at all.

She watched it, then sighed. "I know. Don't feel bad; see how awful I look." The creature wouldn't look at her. "I used to have hair, and now I have none; I'm badly burnt on my head and bruised all over. I'll probably never have hair again," she said sadly.

"You don't have to hide from me. My name is Nil." She put out her hand but then pulled it back quickly; maybe touching it wasn't a very good idea. "What's your name?" She watched the creature cower and shake and drip goo.

"I'll call you Jelly Pain." She looked at it some more. "Did you do something terrible, Jelly Pain? Are you cursed or something? Tell me what happened."

No answer.

"Okay, okay, you don't have to say anything to me." Nil opened the bag around her waist and took out a handful of rose blossoms. She ate one. Nil extended her hand. "Are you hungry? They're delicious rose petals so late in the season."

She ate another blossom and then another, then yawned. "I'm very tired, Jelly Pain."

She still had some rose petals in her hand as she lay down, stretching out on the stone wall and resting her head on it as if it were a pillow. It wasn't long before she was fast asleep.

Some time had gone by when Jelly Pain stood up just enough to peak over the wall and see the sleeping girl. It inched a little closer to her, then closer, then closer still. With its big clumsy hands with the broken fingernails, it reached out to Nil's small, delicate, open hand and, with two thick fingers, took a flower petal. It brought the petal to its mouth and tasted it. Then it reached for another and another and continued to eat until they were all gone.

It moved right up next to the girl. With its wet and gooey hand, it touched Nil's head with an unexpected gentleness. It stroked the girl's head again and this time, where there had been no hair and scabs, there was now brown fuzz and clear skin; the bruises remained, though.

Two hours passed, then Nil opened her eyes. She saw Jelly Pain sitting close to her. She looked at her hand and saw that the rose petals were gone. She sat up. "Did you eat the flowers, Jelly Pain?"

Jelly Pain cowered.

"No, it's perfectly okay. They're good, aren't they?"

Nil rubbed her eyes and her face. She took a deep breath and shrugged her shoulders. For a moment, she thought that Jelly Pain had actually looked at her. "I am running away, Jelly Pain. Would you like to come with me? I am not sure where I'm going, but you are very welcome to join me if you wish." She didn't really know if it understood what she was saying.

Nil got up slowly. "I just have to leave here. I made a mistake coming to Briarwood." She walked to the edge of the clearing. When she turned around, Jelly Pain was walking behind her, making wet squishing sounds with each step. Nil didn't mind the disgusting sound.

"Hey, Jelly Pain, have you ever heard the story of the sea dragon-horse who visited the river goddess, Violet?" Nil asked. "Ruby the fox seemed to like the story, maybe you will too. You want to hear it?"

Now by Nil's side, Jelly Pain squished, squished, squished with each step.

"I'll have to tell you all about Ruby the red fox later; she's the nicest fox I ever met. Do you know any foxes?" she asked, but of course there was no answer, only a blank stare at the ground—but maybe a little less blank. No matter, Nil was happy to just talk to it.

"Come on, lets just walk, and I'll tell you a story. How about that? A long time ago, there was a great warrior sea dragon-horse who went to live in the deepest trench in the ocean because she was so sad. She was heartbroken." Nil looked at the gooey, eye-dropping creature. "Do you know what heartbroken is? I do." Jelly Pain seemed to be listening but had no response.

Nil couldn't tell if it understood her, but it didn't matter; she continued to tell the whole story as she remembered it. They walked along what looked like an old path in the forest in between giant hardwood and pine trees. By the time she got to the part of the story about the sea dragon-horse's tooth falling out of her mouth, Nil's cheeks were very flushed. Her head was hot, but she kept walking. Jelly Pain had stopped.

Nil turned to Jelly Pain, who was watching her.

"Jelly Pain, are you coming or not?" Nil turned and started walking again, but barely; her legs wobbled, then she collapsed to the ground. Her body was burning up with fever. "I can't even become the turtle anymore," she mumbled to herself.

Nil was trembling and shaking. She looked up, and everything was a blur. She could just make out Jelly Pain's image standing over her. "What are you anyway? Poor Jelly Pain, you look so awful . . . but you are so kind and nice to me." Then the little river goddess's vision went black and she was unconscious.

Another two days had passed, and Nub and Penny Boy, moving quickly, were already beyond the same clearing in the pines and the stone-wall circle where Nil had been. The boys followed Sean's map through the Great Forest and into the Valley of the Giants. At a running pace, Nub and Penny Boy stayed alongside the dwindling riverbed and traveled past the mountain of the Great Watcher. All was quiet in the glen—no rumbling of the Great Watcher, no sheep, and no Nil.

Along the way, Nub told Penny Boy all about Nil and about the first time he had seen her at school. He told Penny Boy about White Rice and the turtle. Penny Boy listened to every word.

By the second night, they were far into the Valley of the Giants and still no Nil in sight. Nub decided they should make a camp for a little while and built a warm fire not far from a great towering oak tree. Sitting at the welcoming campfire, Nub took the next to last piece of apple cake out of his pack and unwrapped it. He ate it in just a few bites. For a while the boys sat quietly as the fire crackled and danced.

"Well, good night, Penny Boy," Nub said. "I'm going to close my eyes for a bit." Nub wasn't sure if Penny Boy ever slept. He had never seen him sleeping whenever they stopped to rest. However, Nub knew he had to get some shut-eye, so he lay his head on his pack and fell into a deep, heavy sleep.

With the light of the fire reflecting on Penny Boy's coin head, and sedated by the comforting fire's heat, Penny Boy's eyelids grew heavy. He lay down on the ground under the vast open sky, and he closed his eyes, dropping off to sleep. The shadow of the big oak tree loomed over the sleeping boys.

After the boys had been asleep for a while, the great oak tree creaked. Right in the middle of the tree trunk, a small crack appeared in the bark. The tree creaked again, and the crack grew longer. Creak, creak, creak, the trunk split apart more. A large, thick hand appeared out of the split, followed by a muscular arm. With another sound of splitting wood, the tree trunk cracked open. One lone giant squeezed out from the opening in the wood. He stood about twelve feet tall and was sniffing the air. He had long dark hair and a beard, and he wore a plaid kilt.

By the light of the dwindling fire, the giant tried to focus his long-unused eyes; he saw the two sleeping boys. He sniffed the air again and followed his nose to Nub's backpack, which was under Nub's head. The giant pulled at the backpack, and Nub quickly sat up to see a huge man rummaging through his bag. The giant found the last piece of apple cake. He ate it in one bite, wrapper and all. He looked through the bag again. The giant found an apple. He ate that in one bite too, and then the cheese; now everything to eat was gone.

Dropping the bag to the ground, the giant picked up a good sized log from the ground. *Uhhhh*, Nub held his breath, *are we his next meal?* Ignoring the boy, the giant placed the end of the log in the fire as if it were a matchstick.

Penny Boy sat up.

The giant looked surprised, and he backed away from the campfire. With the fire reflected on Penny Boy's face, maybe the once-cursed giant thought this was a powerful sun god who knows the Great Watcher! Suddenly, the giant was distracted; he sniffed the air as the scent of croggs caught the attention of his hungry stomach. Holding his torch high, he abruptly turned and ran off.

The two boys watched the giant jump into the near-empty riverbed, following the sound of his wet footsteps and the light of his torch until he disappeared into the darkness. Then all was silent again except for the little crackling of the remainder of the flames. Nub stirred the fire and added another two pieces of wood. "Can you believe that, Penny Boy? The giant ate the apple cake and everything else but not us, so I guess we were lucky, huh?" He laughed.

Penny Boy looked at him. If he could have talked, he would have agreed and laughed, too.

At first light, Nub saw the tree that had cracked open. He looked at the rest of the trees in the forest. "Look at that, Penny Boy, there are more giants in those trees! Wow, that's amazing—and creepy."

Nub quickly began packing up. "Come on, we got to go." Nub put his backpack on and kicked dirt onto the smoldering coals of the fire.

They jumped down into the diminishing riverbed and followed it. It led to a tunnel going into the mountain. Now they had to make a choice. There was no turning back once the two boys entered the tunnel. The walls of the tunnel glowed a soft green light due to the tiny illuminated moss that grew on the walls, just as Sean and the pine heads had seen so long ago.

Chapter Twenty

A Very Decent Plan

After being separated from Nub, Robert Snow and White Rice traveled through the forest. Robert Snow did his best to keep them safe from the valley vultures circling overhead and the cave crickets on the ground, all the while carrying Jack Turner's flute—it wasn't easy.

The rat's keen rodent nose led them to some high grasses where they came across Ruby the fox.

"Robert Snow and White Rice, you've come just in the nick of time. They have Jack Turner captive in there," Ruby said in a whisper, pointing to a nearby cave.

Thinking quickly, Robert Snow came up with a plan.

"I heard him yelling at the cave crickets a few hours ago," Ruby told him.

Robert took off his coat and hat—something he almost never did. "In a cave there are rats; it's natural, so they would hardly notice just another rat. Oh, and let's hope they have just eaten."

The plain and naked Robert Snow dashed through the grass and along the edge of the wall that led to the cave. Once beyond the cave entrance, he ran a few feet, then stopped, then another few feet, then stopped, then darted as fast as he could go. He behaved as any normal rat would, not wanting to get caught. He took a chance and ran unnoticed right between a cave cricket's legs; it and another cave cricket were arguing in their shrieking voices. Robert scurried through a maze of junk piles—old toys and clothes, rotting smelling carcasses of sheep and fish, and, oh, rodents of all kinds!

Wiggling his rat whiskers and pointy nose and looking for Jack Turner in all the confusion, Robert spotted the man leaning against the wall. His long, dark hair was matted with blood and dirt, and his face was bloodied, too. His eyes were closed; his hands were tied behind his back. Robert hurried

around and over the mounds of garbage and slipped behind Jack Turner and under his poncho. "Jack Turner! It's me, Robert! Jack Turner! I'm behind you!"

Jack Turner straightened up, hearing the voice of Robert Snow. Robert peeked out from under the poncho. Jack Turner caught sight of him. "Oh, my friend," he whispered, "you look so . . ."

"I know, regular," Robert finished the sentence. "Good to see you, my friend!"

"Yes, you too!" Jack Turner answered. "Get me untied." Under his poncho, Jack felt Robert trying to untie the rope around his wrists, then the rat resorted to skillfully gnawing through it. "Is Nil okay, have you seen her? How's Nub?" Jack Turner asked the rat.

A cave cricket lumbered over to Jack Turner. "Who you talkin' to, old man?" the oversized, primitive bug squeaked. Jack Turner didn't answer.

The cave cricket swiped its claws close to the man's face and caught Jack Turner's cheek, making it bleed from three scratches. "Huh, you'll really have nothin' to say once Asheater gets hold of you! Any minute now."

Jack Turner's hands were free, and he knew that he and Robert Snow must somehow make a run for it. All of a sudden, from outside the cave came flute music. The cave crickets ran to the entrance to see what it was, which made it impossible for Jack Turner and Robert Snow to pass them. Then, down from the hills and out of the tall grasses, like a rescue brigade, came dozens of wild tattooed melon heads.

With the arrival of the melon heads, it was suddenly mayhem inside and outside the cave. The melon heads tripped the cave crickets, jumped on their backs, bit, pinched, and mocked them—all to get the cave crickets to chase them. While the cave crickets were occupied, Jack Turner and Robert Snow made their escape—a dash to the grasses where Ruby had been hiding. But she wasn't there anymore.

Farther away in the woods, Jack Turner saw a horse tied to a tree; it was Old Tom. "Nub must be here," Jack Turner told Robert Snow, and they headed for the tree. That was also where the flute sounds that had alerted the melon heads were coming from.

"Nub," Robert Snow called out.

When they got to the tree, they found Francis Begley playing the flute. At his feet were Ruby and White Rice. Francis stopped playing when he saw Jack Turner. "You're free! Fantastic! The fox's idea worked!"

"Quickly, lets get out of here," said Jack Turner. Taking Old Tom's reigns, they headed for the hollowed-out log just above the waterfall, which was now barely falling.

"Thank you, Francis," said Jack Turner. "What are you doing here?"

"I'm looking for Nub. He is missing, along with Nil. Terrible things are happening in town; we must find them. Anyway, I came across the fox, Ruby, who asked if I played the flute. I have never spoken with a fox before. She told me the details, and asked if I could help, so here I am."

Ruby cleared her throat, "Em . . . em . . . I saw Nil here by the waterfall maybe three days ago. She had been attacked by that horrible monster. She was leaving the river and looked so, so sad." The fox bowed her head.

"I was with Nub just last night," said Robert. "Until that man, who smells like cigars and—"

"Devlin!" Jack Turner and Francis said together.

"And he knocked Nub down. He had a big knife, I'm afraid. He's looking for the book."

"Yes, I know," said Jack Turner.

"I'm afraid he might have gotten it. Nub had it in his backpack," Robert said regretfully.

"What book?" Francis asked.

"It's a very special, old green book, but we'll get to that later," Jack Turner said.

"I know that book. It was once here, hidden in the log. I saw it with my own eyes. Penny Boy found it," said Francis Begley.

Robert Snow looked at him. "How could that be?"

"There *is* a lot to talk about. Nub doesn't know, does he Francis?" Jack Turner asked.

"No, he doesn't. I was waiting for the right moment, but it never seemed to come," replied Francis.

Jack Turner looked down at Robert Snow. "Francis Begley is Dusty Miller."

"Jack Turner found me when I was nearly dead and brought me to the Begleys. They took care of me and adopted me; no one ever knew but Jack Turner—and Gina, of course, Nub's mother."

Robert Snow's little jaw dropped open. "Really! And Ash is your brother?"

Francis Begley's face said everything without words. The pain over his lost brother haunted him. He still loved his brother, despite everything. "Yes," he replied, "so sad. The truth is, I wasn't just looking for Nub; I've also been through the woods looking for Ash. I hoped maybe he would remember me."

Old Tom stirred and picked his head up; he flattened his ears.

"Maybe that's Ash," Francis Begley said in a hush.

"Careful, Francis, I think he's too far gone," Jack Turner warned him.

They heard heavy footsteps and voices coming out of the woods.

Quickly leading Old Tom, Francis Begley, Ruby, Jack Turner carrying White Rice, and Robert Snow moved away to the thick patch of holly bushes, but they were barely hidden from sight.

The crunching sounds got closer and from the trees stepped a hideous creature. It went toward the hollowed-out log, looking for the tooth. Again he was ordered by the persistent voice from his skin, "Find it, Mr. Page, find it now!"

At the sight of Mr. Page, Old Tom snorted and stamped his hoof on the ground. Mr. Page looked up and saw the horse and the rest of them. "Ignore them, Mr. Page! Find it!" But Mr. Page was easily frightened. The creature straightened up, which seemed painful because he screeched in a loud whine, and ran awkwardly back into the woods.

"Dear God, what is that thing?" asked Francis.

Jack Turner spoke. "That is, was, Devlin. He obviously found the book and has been cursed by it. Nub had the book last, Francis, so that means . . ."

"That means Nub is in serious danger!" Francis replied. "Which way was Nub headed when you last saw him?" he asked Robert Snow.

Robert Snow pointed in the direction of the Miller property.

"I'll take Old Tom and head to the old house," said Francis.

Jack Turner picked up White Rice. "I'll head back to my house and then come to the farm, Francis: maybe Nub or Nil have come back. I'll see you tonight. Coming, Robert?" Jack Turner asked the rat.

"I'll come to the Begley farm tonight. I'll stay here with Ruby for a while and nose around," Robert said. "This seems to be a popular meeting place."

"Okay then, we'll meet later."

When Jack Turner returned to his house, he found the mess that Devlin had made while looking for the old green book; there was no sign of Nil or Nub.

Francis Begley rode Old Tom to the big Miller house he had once known as home. He was aghast to find in the kitchen the collapsed cupboard that had been moved and now revealed a door he had never known existed. He went through the door and made his way down the long dark hallway to the open round, metal door. Looking down, with the aid of the dim light through little cracked window, he saw the old blanket and other things that looked familiar. In horror, he realized that Penny Boy had been hidden here all those years. All the times he had come to look for his friend, he had been right here under his nose! He called out for his son or Penny Boy, not knowing that they had found each other.

The house was vacant and quiet; the black mold all but dried up and the soul crawlers dead. Francis stopped by the old, fallen-down greenhouse. For a hopeful moment, he thought he might find his son or Penny Boy waiting for him, but they weren't.

Francis Begley rode Old Tom off the Miller property, past Jack Turner's house and the abandoned Briarwood Inn, then back to the farm to tell Gina the dismal news.

As for Robert Snow, quite some time after Jack Turner and Francis Begley had left, he was sitting on the hollowed-out log, all dressed again, listening to Ruby tell about Nil's visit with her, when something caught his attention on the ground. There, drawn in the dirt, was the symbol of the Great Watcher and an arrow pointing in the direction away from Briarwood. "Ah! Nub has left me a sign!" He stood up. "Ruby, I must leave you and go that way." He pointed. "Tell Jack Turner and Mr. Begley, if you see them, that I have headed north. I have a hunch."

Robert Snow quickly scurried down the path along the river; he was the only one who had known that the sea dragon-horse's tooth was hidden underneath the symbol on the cover of the green book. He was to have given it to Nil when it was time. This had been his promise to Violet.

Chapter Twenty-One

Into the Valley of the Giants

J elly Pain had picked up Nil when she collapsed and carried the sick river goddess, with uncanny strength, for two days. It took her into the Valley of the Giants and through the dimly lit tunnel. By the time they reached the opening at the other side of the mountain, Nil was feverish and weak, and her heartbeat was dangerously rapid. Jelly Pain continued to travel upriver for several hours.

Through a veil of soft mist, the tall, green outlines of the great pines and hardwoods that made up this ancient river-goddess forest could be seen. Thick green moss covered the rocks and tree trunks, and ferns covered the ground.

Jelly Pain came to a bend in the river where there was a small hut made of mud and straw; next to the hut was a great willow tree. All around the base of the tree and around the hut grew tiny, dark-purple violets. Jelly Pain took Nil into the hut and put her down on a thick, soft, grass mat in front of the fireplace. There were very few things inside the hut—cups and bowls, sticks, and some pots—and it smelled of sweet-grass and thyme.

Outside the hut, Jelly Pain gathered wood, then brought it inside and put it in the stone hearth. Jelly Pain rubbed two sticks together, careful not to drip goo on them, and a tiny flame appeared; gradually, a fire grew in the fireplace.

Taking the bark of the willow tree, some willow leaves, and the darkest-purple violet blossoms, Jelly Pain mashed them in a bowl, then added some river water. Jelly Pain cooked this mixture in a pot over the fire. It boiled, and the steam rose into the air; Nil breathed it in. All that evening, through the night, and all the next day, Jelly Pain fed Nil the willow/violet tea and kept the fire going. Nil slept by the fire.

Faint whispers could be heard outside the hut. All around, grass goblins had gathered. They looked through the doorway and windows and watched the proceedings. They talked quietly amongst themselves so as to not disturb her sleep. Stony creatures came from farther away—they tried to be quiet, too.

"She is very sick, don't you think?" one grass goblin asked another.

"Did you see? The river is sick, too."

"Are you sure that's Nil? Her hair looks funny, and she's all bruised. Something's wrong with her."

"I hope it can help her," the stony creature said of Jelly Pain.

That night, the light of a half moon poured through the hut window and onto Nil's feverish body like a soothing shower. The grass goblins and stony creatures slept outside, vigilant of the river goddess.

Through the night, Nil struggled within her body, fretting and distressed as when she had pulled herself out of the turtle shell. She tossed and twisted, and Jelly Pain comforted her, wiping her brow with a willow/violet tea–soaked rag. Eventually, she seemed to calm down.

Nil had a dream. In the dream, she was swimming in the river. She saw a tiny blue crab floating on the surface. It looked

like it was waving to her with its little front claw, like it was calling to her to follow—*to find my turtle shell*, Nil thought. Then the crab dove under the water and was gone. Nil looked around, but there was nothing except vast water for miles and miles and no sign of land.

Uhh, I'm in the ocean not the river, Nil realized. She put her head below the surface to look for the crab and saw the little crustacean swimming downward. Nil followed it all the way down, into the darkest green- and blue-colored water she had ever seen. Down, down, down to the very bottom. To her delight, Nil could walk along the sandy bottom on the ocean floor; with the help of the glowing fish and shrimp that swam by like little flashlights, she could kind of see.

Nil saw something large—maybe a big coral rock or a ship-wreck?—lying on the bottom. When she approached it, she saw it was something else. Nil touched it. The surface of it was rough and hard. *A whale!* Nil thought. The creature moved under her touch and raised its head to look right at Nil. Nil stared and stared, studying its face and eyes, its mouth, its big teeth. Nil could see all the big pointy teeth, but there was an empty space; one of the teeth was missing. She couldn't believe it. She was standing in front of the sea dragon-horse!

Nil wanted to speak to her, but no words would come out. The sea dragon-horse didn't say anything either. Nil wanted to tell her so much: who she was, that she was Nil and her mother was Violet, that she was the river goddess who was the turtle, and that her father was a mortal man named Daniel. She wanted so badly to tell her that she knew the sea dragon-horse's story and about the tooth she had given to her mother, but she couldn't speak. It was as if she had forgotten how to talk. *Maybe it's because I'm underwater or maybe I've* lost my ability to speak. Oh, no! Without my shell, without the river, I'm forgetting how to talk! And why won't the sea dragon-horse talk to me? Maybe it's because the sea dragon-horse is angry or disappointed in me for not being courageous, for leaving my turtle shell. Nil needed to speak to her; it was urgent. She wanted to tell the sea dragon-horse that she was not courageous, that she was scared. Nil felt as if she would explode if something didn't happen soon.

Then something did happen; the sea dragon-horse slowly opened its big mouth until it was wide open. Nil looked into the big mouth, past the big pointy teeth, and into a dark abyss as inky as the blackest sky at night. What am I supposed to see? she thought. Am I supposed to ask her a question? Now is my only chance to ask it, but I can't speak. Where is my voice? I have lost it forever, I think. Say something, Nil! Say something; your life depends on it! Or maybe I'm already dead!

Suddenly, Nil woke up; she was lying on her side on the grass mat in the hut. She was soaking wet. Had the high fever broken, or had she been swimming in the ocean—or both?

She squinted her eyes against the bright morning light coming in the windows and open doorway. She raised herself to her elbows and looked around the empty room. The fire was out, and the coals were grey and barely warm. How long have I been here? Through the open window, she spied a grass goblin that was peeking in at her.

"She's awake!" Nil heard the grass goblin whisper outside the window.

"I'm awake," she heard herself say, and she was very happy to hear her voice; she still could talk.

"Uhh, did you hear that? The river goddess spoke," said a stony creature, and it popped its head up to look at her.

"Hi," Nil said.

Four grass goblins and three stony creatures went around to the open doorway and were just about to enter. Then the sound of footsteps could be heard coming toward the hut. The grass goblins and stony creatures ran for cover, disappearing behind trees, up onto the branches, or into the grass lumps. Some of the stony creatures jumped into the almost empty riverbed and disguised themselves as river rocks.

Nub and Penny Boy appeared at the doorway and looked at Nil on the grass mat. "Nil, Nil!" Nub smiled, quickly went into the hut, and knelt down next to her.

"Nub!" she answered, "And . . . ?" she looked at Penny Boy.

"And Penny Boy," Nub told her.

"Penny Boy," Nil repeated. "Hi," she said to him.

Penny Boy just stared at her and stayed shyly by the doorway. He had never met a girl before, and this girl had so little hair that she could almost have passed for a Penny Girl.

"I must have come through the tunnel last night. I don't remember, but I'm in my mother's land, I believe," she told him.

"In your land too, Nil," Nub reminded her.

"Jack Turner told you, then," she said.

He nodded. "Yes, he did."

She looked around. "Where's Jelly Pain?"

"Who?" Nub asked.

"Jelly Pain. It took care of me." Nil looked around. "Jelly Pain," she called out, but there was no sign of it.

"I don't know," said Nub. "We haven't seen anyone or anything since we came out of the tunnel. It seems empty here."

Nil smiled. "Oh, it's not; trust me on that. It's good to see you Nub." Nil took his hand and held it to her cheek.

"You too, Nil," he answered and kissed her hand.

Nil smiled. Her eyes filled with tears.

Still holding her hand, Nub helped her up. Nil was pale and just a little bit of hair grew on her head, but beside that and the bruises on her head and face, she was doing all right.

"I want to go outside and look around to see if I can find Jelly Pain," Nil said.

Holding Nub's hand, she walked out the door past Penny Boy. She looked around at the great trees in their moss coats, at the ferns that covered the ground, and at the dark-purple violets. She went to the river by the great big willow tree and stopped. Looking down into the river, she saw that only a puddle here and there remained. "The river is leaving because I did, isn't it?"

"Maybe. Probably. Yeah, I'm pretty sure that's what's happening," Nub replied. "So don't leave, Nil; come back with us."

All three of them were now looking down at the vacant riverbed. Nub was about to tell her about Jack Turner when he noticed tears running down Nil's cheeks. "What is it?" Nub asked.

Nil looked at him. She was reluctant to say, as if telling made it true and more unbearable. "I . . . I'm not the turtle anymore. After that monster thing attacked me, I left the shell below the waterfall. I don't think I'm a river goddess anymore. How could I be? I think it's too late. Look, the river is proof."

"You can go back and get it. I'm . . . I bet it's there right now," Nub said.

"And the golden carp died because of me, because I did that," Nil said.

Nub put his hand in his pocket. "Look what I have!"

"The tooth! You have the sea dragon-horse tooth. That's amazing, Nub! I dreamed about her," Nil recalled. "I saw the missing space in her mouth, but she wouldn't talk to me. I thought she was mad at me for doing what I did. For not being courageous like her and my mother."

"Nil, it's yours now; here." Nub handed her the tooth. She held it in her open hand looking at it and crying.

"Yes you do," said Nub.

"Yes, I do what?" she asked him.

"Have the courage," he answered. "Nil, listen to me; this tooth fell out of the cover of the green book. The book is gone, I'm afraid; it kind of exploded. And it's sort of my fault. The book was stolen from my pack, but then I found this tooth after the book was destroyed. And believe me, the man who took the book is cursed. You were right." Nub smiled at her. "Maybe this can help you, Nil."

"Yes, maybe it can," she agreed, with a spark of strength.

"Even if you're not the turtle anymore," he added. "Oh!" he remembered more good news. "Nil, White Rice found me at the farm! Can you believe that? She is with Robert Snow!"

Nil kissed his cheek. "You are magic!"

"Well, I don't know about that." He blushed.

"Thank you, Nub," Nil said. "I wish I could say goodbye to Jelly Pain, but . . ."

"So you're coming back?" Nub smiled.

Nil nodded. "Yes, Ruby was right all along. I have to."

Nil went inside the hut, retrieved her little bag, and tied it around her waist.

They walked in the grass beside the riverbed. The mist had lifted, the air was clear, and the sky was blue; much different from the thick cloud cover that hung over the river around

Briarwood. Nil looked around and remembered the forest well—the trees, bushes, plants, and flowers. There were beech, hickory, elm, and giant, thousand-year-old sycamore trees, some of which were more than one hundred and fifty feet tall and twenty-five feet around. There were towering tulip trees, sugar maples, black oak, and white oak. There were clusters of red-flowering spicebushes and yellow witch hazel bushes, wild ferns, and blue, pink, and purple violets. Moving through a section of ancient pines and evergreen trees, Nil remembered the smells of the forest: the dried pine needles and the bark with drips of pine tar. She passed the great giant rocks, placed there by the glaciers of long ago, where she recalled playing with grass goblins. The woods were a part of her as much as the river that ran through her.

"Jack Turner is missing, Nil." Nub broke into her reverie. "At least, he was when I left. I found his flute by the pool below the waterfall, but I dropped it. I think Robert Snow has it now."

Nil didn't say anything. Her dear friend Jack Turner mattered to her so much; he had played the flute to find her, and now he was missing.

"It must be hard to be a river goddess, Nil," Nub said, feeling the weight she was carrying.

"I'll find him. I have to," she said.

"*We'll* find him," Nub told her.

Nil took Nub's arm. "Thanks, Nub."

Nub looked at Penny Boy, who was walking along a little behind them. "We like stories, don't we, Penny Boy?" Nub asked him.

Penny Boy nodded yes.

"Do you think Nil should tell us the story of the dragon-horse tooth?" he asked Penny Boy.

Penny Boy caught up to Nil and Nub.

"She was a *sea* dragon-horse, actually. Okay, okay." Nil giggled. "This will be the third time I've told this story," she said, as they climbed down into the riverbed to follow it to the tunnel entrance in the mountain.

Nil started from the beginning. "A very long time ago, a great warrior sea dragon-horse came to visit my mother, Violet, the river goddess. For a long, long time, she had lived down in the deepest trench of the ocean in the dark . . ."

While Nil told the story, Penny Boy did not blink his eyes even once. He listened raptly to every word. By the time she finished the part about the tooth falling out, the three of them were walking side by side. Penny Boy knew what it was like to live in isolation and darkness, that was for sure. He was happy to hear about the little blue crab and glowing things that swam by the sea dragon-horse. He remembered the spider that had kept him company for so many years and the night he had heard the music.

"Look!" said Nub pointing.

There was the tunnel entrance.

"Hey, do you hear that?" asked Nub. "Is that thunder or what? Do you feel that? Is it an earthquake?"

"I don't think so," answered Nil, "but it's something."

The ground trembled.

"Maybe it's the Great Watcher!" exclaimed Nil.

The ground shook harder and the sound got closer and louder. Then, right in front of them, the giant leaped into the riverbed and almost crushed them. It seemed not to even notice the three of them and disappeared into the tunnel entrance a little ahead of them.

"That was the giant we saw last night," Nub told Nil.

"Would you believe he came out of a tree and ate all of our food? I think it was the apple cake he smelled."

"Wish we had some now," said Nil.

"Okay, apple cake it is when we get back," said Nub, optimistically.

Nil took a deep breath. She loved the idea of a happy time with apple cake and Nub and Penny Boy in Briarwood, but there was great peril she would have to face before that and a test that she was not sure she was up to.

The tunnel still glowed with the soft-green hue from the moss. "Oh, that moss is beautiful," Nil commented. "I remember that from when I was—" she stopped. "Well, a long time ago with Robert Snow."

"You are good friends, aren't you?" Nub asked her.

"Yes, we are. In many ways, he is my guardian."

Nub smiled at that idea. He was very fond of Robert Snow, too.

They walked along quietly for a while. Nil would have loved to know something about Penny Boy, what he was or where he came from—things like that. So would Nub, for that matter, but the coin-headed boy couldn't speak. Maybe someday Penny Boy could write it down for them, but that would have to wait.

They had been walking for hours and Nil and Nub were hungry. Penny Boy tapped Nil on the shoulder. He pointed to a patch of small white mushrooms growing in the dirt of the tunnel. How could he have known what they were feeling?

"Oh, Penny Boy! White button mushrooms!" Nil quickly picked some. She handed one to Nub and started to give one to Penny Boy but stopped when she remembered that he didn't have a mouth. "Besides roses and pine nuts, and probably apple cake, mushrooms are my favorite," she told them as she ate one after another, "Robert Snow says they are such a humble little mushroom." She giggled.

Nub ate several, too.

"Thank you, Penny Boy," Nil said. Then they resumed their journey.

After walking for what seemed like days, they saw light at the end of the tunnel. They ran down the riverbed and out into the valley. Downriver a bit, Nub showed Nil the camp that he and Penny Boy had made, and he showed her the trees of giants and the cracked-open one from which the one giant had escaped.

"Robert Snow has told me of these giants who were punished by the Great Watcher, but if I were the Great Watcher, I would end the curse," Nil said, touching the bark of the trees.

"Me, too," said Nub.

Penny Boy nodded as if to say, "So would I."

"It's crazy to think that apple cake could break a curse, don't you think?" Nil asked.

"Yeah, it is," Nub agreed. "But maybe it wasn't the apple cake, then." He thought about it.

"Then what did it, do you think?" asked Nil.

They looked at Penny Boy as if he had the answer, but he shrugged his shoulders.

"Hmm," said Nil. "I wonder." Struck by a thought, she looked at Nub. "Uhhh . . . maybe the curse is over. Maybe the giants are waking up now! It's possible. Come on, maybe the Great Watcher is here. Come on, lets go see," she called out, as they hurried down the valley.

Chapter Twenty-Two

The Quest Continues

As they approached the mountain of the Great Watcher, all was quiet; there was no sign of him. Penny Boy pointed to a very tiny figure walking toward them.

"That's Robert Snow," announced Nil. The three of them hurried toward the rat.

"Robert Snow!" Nil bent down and kissed and hugged him so much that his hat fell off, and he was lifted off the ground, "It's so good to see you!" she said.

Penny Boy handed Robert his hat. "This is Penny Boy, Robert; he was at the Millers' house," Nub said.

"Ah, yes, the little boy who found the book in the log a long time ago. I remember you," Robert Snow told Penny Boy. "Hello there."

Penny Boy looked at the rat with his big eyes and was happy to have all these new friends.

The rat was straightening his hat when he noticed Nil's condition. "Oh, my dear." He sounded very concerned.

"I know, my hair; but look, it's growing back," Nil reassured her friend.

"Nil." Robert Snow took her hand. "I have something to tell you." He seemed worried.

"Have you seen Jack Turner? Is he okay?" asked Nub.

"Yes, yes," Robert answered. "He was well when I left him. And so was White Rice, thanks to Francis Begley, your father."

"My father?"

"Yes, your father went looking for you on Old Tom and found Ruby the fox who had Jack Turner's flute. Your father played the flute and the melon heads came, which helped me and Jack Turner escape from the cave crickets before Asheater arrived. It was brilliant!"

"My father did that?" Nub said in astonishment. "I didn't know he had it in him."

There is much Nub doesn't know about his father, thought Robert Snow, but it was not for him to tell at this time.

"Oh, Robert," Nil blurted out, barely containing herself and interrupting Robert's thoughts and Nub's further questioning. "You cannot believe what Nub found!" She reached in her bag and pulled out a mushroom.

"Oh, how delicious," Robert Snow commented and was happy to take the mushroom.

"No! Not that." Nil laughed. "This!" She reached in again and revealed the sea dragon-horse tooth.

Robert Snow was nearly knocked off his paws. This was what he had been wanting to talk to her about. How he had lost the tooth before he could give it to her as her mother had wanted. The rat stood speechless; his keen brown eyes grew wider. He reached out to touch the tooth in Nil's hand, as if he had to touch it to believe it was real.

"Oh, I can't tell you how incredible this is!" Robert Snow said. "I was supposed to give this to you. Your mother had asked me to. I was waiting for the right time, but I lost it. I thought that I had failed you and that now it was too late. Oh! I am so happy! Thank you, Nub!"

Nub smiled and Penny Boy took in the important moment. It felt so right and good to have the four of them together.

"Now we must travel back in haste," said Robert Snow. "Keep that safe, Nil."

Nil put the sea dragon-horse tooth back in her waist bag, and they determinedly continued their journey. But in the shadow of the mountain of the Great Watcher, Nil stopped, her head hanging down, looking at her feet as if she could not go on.

The other three travelers looked at her.

"What is it?" Robert Snow asked. "What's wrong? We must hurry! Don't you feel well?"

She was reluctant to tell Robert, of all people. Her eyes were full of tears. "I don't deserve the sea dragon-horse tooth. I gave up the turtle shell. It's not a part of me anymore. So I'm not the river goddess anymore, even with the tooth. I've been thinking, the only hope I have is that the river doesn't depend on me being the river goddess."

Robert listened and was thoughtful. "From all that I know and what was written in the green book, the river and the river goddess are one. It is apparent that the river is evaporating into the sky. So, let's get you back and hope for the best. Come on now, let's go with the courage of Sean the rabbit thief," Robert encouraged them. "Let me remind you of the rabbit's exceptional courage and humility." And Robert Snow briefly told them the story of Sean's race to win the river. Nil knew it, of course, but Nub and Penny Boy were fascinated.

By late afternoon, they were leaving the valley and approaching the Great Forest. They passed the stone wall where Nil had met Jelly Pain. She told them about the creature, how awful it looked but how wonderful it had been to her. "Someday I'll come back to find Jelly Pain," Nil said.

"I know we need to get back as soon as possible, but the night will soon be here. This looks like a good place to make a nice campfire, rest a bit, and enjoy those mushrooms," Robert Snow suggested. They all agreed.

While they sat around the fire in the center of the stone-wall circle, eating mushrooms and pine nuts, Robert Snow spoke. "Now that you know the story, you may be amazed to learn that this is the very place where Sean the rabbit thief told the animals of the troubled forest that he would go find Violet, Nil's mother, and win the river for them."

They could almost see Jimmy the squirrel sitting on the tree branch above them or Finn, the bear with one ear, with his medical bag and honey cakes or cranky Edward the eagle complaining about the impossibility of the situation.

The four of them were quiet, watching the movement of the fire, one of the things the animals of the troubled forest couldn't have. If the river disappeared for good, a fire would soon be too dangerous again.

"He did it for Meeka," Nil said suddenly. "Sean loved her."

"Ahhhh, yes, he did it for love," confirmed Robert Snow, "one of the greatest causes of all causes."

"What are other causes?" asked Nub. "Justice?"

"Yes, justice is one," Robert told him.

"Robert, tell us one of the poems you said to Sean when he was at the end of the valley; you know, where the giants are cursed inside the trees," Nil requested.

"Ah, yes. Well, Sean had just received the tattoo from the Great Watcher on his ear the day before, and he had fallen asleep on the back of the sheep in a great snow storm. He awoke to a valley covered with snow."

"Oh, I'd like to see snow!" said Nil.

"The Great Watcher, knowing of Sean's promise, sent me to greet him. I spoke these words:

> "An opening to such a place
> of magic, love, and of grace,
> there's no such thing as a race
> to find or win such a river!
>
> A heart that sings is the only key,
> a heart of courage and humility;
> on this matter trust in me
> to find such a river!"

"Oh, I love that one," Nil said.

"What was the song he sang, Robert?" Nil asked, reminiscing.

"A song that Sean was almost too shy to sing, but a hero

who sings . . . well, good fortune will follow, I like to say. It is always that way," Robert informed them. "With encouragement from the pine heads, Sean did sing, and it went like this:

"A river runs from you to me
This river runs for eternity
A silent promise never broken
Of true love, so sweetly spoken
A heart that beats for you and me
One pure heart for eternity
A world like ours is never broken
With my song, like wings, now open!"

They all clapped, even Penny Boy, and although the clouds hung heavy in the night sky over the empty riverbed, the group was uplifted and a lightness could be felt in the air.

"Robert, how many years ago was that?" Nub asked.

"Ah," responded Robert, turning his long pointy nose to the sky, "seems like yesterday, but it wasn't; time is funny like that."

More curious, Nub asked another question. "What happened to the Great Watcher?"

"I don't know; I haven't seen him or felt his rumbles. Now that there are no more sheep in the valley, he seems to have gone to sleep."

"Speaking of giants," Nub said, "one of them broke out of the trees back there in the valley and ate my apple cake and everything else in my bag. Then he ran through the mountain tunnel and, later, back out again."

Robert Snow listened with great interest, "Hmmm, a waking giant; awakened by apple cake, imagine that," was all he said before changing the subject. "Maybe we all should get some sleep. We need our rest."

They saw that Nil had already fallen asleep. "Good night boys," said Robert.

"Good night," answered Nub. Penny Boy just closed his eyes; then all was quiet.

A little while after they were all asleep, a group of pine heads whispered quietly. They hung with their large hands and long, skinny arms from a tree branch above the sleeping group. Then they stealthily dropped from the branch to the soft pine needles on the ground and quickly made their way to Nub's bag, opening it. They were sure they would find some sweet foods, like honey cakes. Some things just don't change. They rummaged through the backpack, pulling everything out, including Penny Boy's metal box. They fiddled with the latch until the box opened. "Mmm, looks like seeds," one of them whispered, and they began to eat them by the handful, stuffing them into their mouths, spilling some of them onto the ground. Then a strong whirl of wind blew by them and—swoosh!—all the remaining seeds flew into the air and were carried away. The metal box was empty.

Hours passed and the early morning light woke Penny Boy. He sat up and saw the empty metal box; next to it slept five pine heads—the guilty parties.

Penny Boy took the metal box into his lap. He looked closely in one corner where just a seed or two remained stuck. He had kept the seeds safe for more than twenty years, and now they were gone. He tried to scoop up a few of the spilled seeds and put them back in the box, but it was mostly just dirt.

Nub woke up and saw Penny Boy with the empty box and his backpack turned over with all the contents pulled out. Then he saw sleeping the pine heads, their hands covered with seeds.

Robert Snow awakened to see what was happening.

"Whatever those creatures are, they ate all the seeds in the box. They were Penny Boy's," Nub told him. "He's kept them for a long time."

"Ah, those are pine heads," said Robert.

The pine heads heard the rat's voice and woke up.

"Robert Snow!" they all said in unison.

"How do you know me?" he asked.

"Ollabell and Stan told us all about you and the rabbit thief. You are famous!"

Robert Snow laughed at that comment, at the silliness of the idea of him being famous. "Sean was legendary, indeed," he said humbly. "Ollabell and Stan, I remember them well. Are they still here, by chance?"

"No, I'm afraid not," one of them answered, "but we are related to them," he said proudly.

"Ah, wonderful, but now I must ask you to apologize to Penny Boy for eating something you shouldn't have." Robert pointed to the empty metal box.

The pine heads just stared at Penny Boy with wide eyes, unable to say a word.

From behind Penny Boy, Nil sat up. "Ohhh, the little river goddess," said one of the pine heads, and they all forgot that they were supposed to say that they were sorry!

"Pine heads!" exclaimed Nil, getting to her feet. "What have you done now?"

"Oh, your hair has disappeared like the river water," said one of the pine heads.

"Shhhh . . ." said another pine head, nudging the first pine head and knocking him over.

"Oh, never mind that," Nil told them. "What can you tell us. Have you seen anything or anyone?"

Just then, big shadows crossed the sky. At least twenty valley vultures flew over the tops of the pine trees; their wings clipped the treetops and shook them.

"I think we have been spotted," said Nub.

"We must hurry now!" Robert commanded.

"Oh, please, may I come with you?" one of the pine heads asked.

"And me too," said another.

"Can they ride on the pack with me, Nub?" Robert asked the boy.

"Of course! What are your names?" he asked the pine heads who wanted to go along.

"I'm Frieda," said the first.

"And I'm her brother Scott," said the other.

"Yes, yes, hurry up," said Robert.

Nub was quickly gathering his stuff and repacking the backpack. He put the metal box, with the few seeds Penny Boy had rescued, into the pack, too. Then Nub scooped up the pine heads and Robert Snow and placed them on top of the backpack.

"To the waterfall . . . well, what's left of it," said Robert.

"Yes! That's where I left my turtle shell," said Nil.

Lawrence, Diana, and Homer, the other three pine heads, bade them farewell.

"I have an idea how to help," Lawrence whispered to the other two pine heads. Diana and Homer nodded in agreement.

Chapter Twenty-Three

The Great Rain Battle

Since first light, Jack Turner had been standing at the edge of the empty pool under the all but vanished Jumping Grace Waterfall. The rocky face was now just a cliff again, like in the days of the troubled forest. Desperately, Jack Turner played his flute in hopes that it would help the only remaining water elemental, who was dying. Ruby the fox stood by his legs, next to her was White Rice. Below them, in the tiny puddle that remained, lay the once-powerful water elemental, now a small and helpless water puppy, just minutes from evaporating into oblivion.

On the rocks, on the cliffs overhead, and all around the surrounding area sat more than a hundred glum, wild melon heads. They had been attracted by the music and now watched the puddle and listened to Jack Turner play, waiting for some kind of miracle. Some of the melon heads nervously bit their nails, a bad habit they had picked up in recent times.

A melon head at the edge of the cliff stood up to sniff the

air. Then, several more melon heads stood and sniffed the air. Something was coming closer.

Noticing them, Jack Turner stopped playing to listen. They could hear footsteps crunching in the dead leaves. Everyone hoped it wasn't cave crickets. Ruby the fox ran up the steep path at the side of the cliff to look.

"Be careful," Jack Turner whispered to her. Before Ruby could even reach the top, the melon heads starting jumping up and down. Coming down the path were Nil, Penny Boy, and Nub, who carried Robert Snow and the pine heads on his backpack.

They reached the edge of the cliff, looked over, and waved happily to Jack Turner. But the smiles were quick to leave their faces when they saw what was lying in the empty pool below; what was once the tremendous, fierce, water elemental was now a small puddle of a creature. Nil quickly climbed down the path. Nub and Penny Boy followed. With no time for hellos, Nil jumped down to the pool where what was left of the water elemental lay. She touched it with her hand. "I'm here, it's me, Nil." But the water elemental didn't respond to her voice.

Nil looked up at the group standing along the edge, then looked around at the empty riverbed floor; there was no sign of her turtle shell anywhere. "Well, my turtle shell is gone, and the water elemental is almost gone, too. Just look at it," Nil said sadly to Nub, who had bent down next to her.

"What if you could make it rain? The river water is in the clouds," Nub said, pointing to the heavy ribbon of thick clouds that hung over them.

"It won't rain just 'cause I want it to, Nub."

"Nil, you have the sea dragon-horse tooth. It's sharp, and it's a powerful charm. Put the tooth in the elemental's little paw, and we'll throw it to the clouds. If it could cut one of the clouds open with the sharp edge, maybe it will rain."

"We can try," Nil said. "Hang on," she whispered to the little, fading water puppy. "Hold this tooth"

The little watery paw clutched the tooth.

"We're going to throw you in the air, and when I say cut, try to cut the cloud open," Nil said. "It was a great warrior's tooth, and you're a warrior, too."

Together Nub and Nil held the water puppy. They would have to throw it far up to reach the clouds, and they'd have to catch it when it came down, or it would just splat into drops of liquid.

"Okay, ready? One, two, three!" They tossed the little figure into the air as high as they could. As it got close to the clouds, Nil yelled, "Cut!"

It raised his tiny paw and made a slice, but it hadn't reached the clouds. It fell down into Nub and Nil's arms.

Penny Boy climbed down into the riverbed and approached Nub and Nil. He added his strength to Nub and Nil's.

"Okay, let's try again," said Nub.

"Now, one, two, three, and throw!" called Nub, and they heaved the little water being into the sky again. Its little paw raised the tooth and swiped at the clouds; a small tear appeared.

One, two, three, four raindrops fell from the rip in the cloud and splashed onto the water elemental. It twitched. Then another big raindrop fell and splashed.

"Again!" they said, and threw the creature a third time, even higher into the clouds. "Cut!" called Nil, and again it sliced at the cloud with the tooth. This time it made a bigger tear and several big raindrops fell onto it and into the dry pool below.

More raindrops fell on the water elemental, and it grew to double its size.

Nil, Nub, and Penny Boy tossed it for the fourth time. It was able to make a much larger slash this time, and raindrops of river water poured from the cloud. Now that it was getting soaked, the water elemental grew four times its size. Then ten times, and so on.

With its strength back, the water elemental could leap up to the cloud cover, cutting more and more slices. The rain fell even harder. Also from the clouds fell wiggling spotted trout and leaping frogs.

Then ever larger drops of water fell from the openings. Inside the big drops were some very unusual creatures, all new to the Yawning Rabbit River; no one there had ever seen anything like them before. They were rain people. When they hit the ground and the raindrop popped like a bubble bursting, they ran crazily all around the pool. They were human looking, in some ways—they had long black hair swirled upward, muscular legs and arms—but they only stood about eight to twelve inches tall. They had pale, naked bodies; elfish faces with big, dark eyes, small mouths, pointy noses, and big, pointy fairy ears; and long pointy devilish tails. Their feet and hands were more like claws.

Suddenly, a brilliant, emerald-green, triple lightning bolt shot from the sky and struck the ground, shaking it. The lightning burned a large mark in the grass, but it wasn't a mark at all; they were letters: K B T. Through the opening in the clouds, a figure dropped out, riding the air on strange metal shoes. As he approached the ground, the man glided and landed alongside the riverbed, right on top of the three letters. The man stood on the riverbank on the opposite side, across from Jack Turner.

He was a tall thin man, dressed in a very peculiar fashion for the times, but he was familiar to Nub.

He had long black hair, a handlebar mustache, and a funny beard. He wore a black derby hat, goggles like an old-fashioned pilot, and a western-looking gun and holster. His thin muscular arms were covered in tattoos similar to those on the wild melon heads, and on his feet were the flying, cosmic metal shoes.

It was Kurt Burning Trail!

Penny Boy's eyes couldn't have been bigger.

"You really exist?!" exclaimed Nub.

"Of course I do," answered Kurt Burning Trail. "Hey, Turner!" Kurt Burning Trail yelled across the riverbed. "Got your message for help. Came as soon as I could."

"Thanks, Kurt, I appreciate it; we're in a mess all right," answered Jack Turner.

"Yeah, well, it's worse than you know; the ghost hunters have arrived with their molfs. I've been tracking them for weeks; a troubled town with a monster problem is their kind 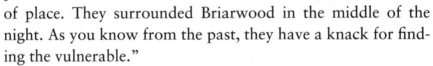 of place. They surrounded Briarwood in the middle of the night. As you know from the past, they have a knack for finding the vulnerable."

Nub still couldn't believe he was looking at the real Kurt Burning Trail; that he was a friend of Jack Turner's was even more amazing. "Does that gun really shoot bla—"

"Black bat and spider spit," Kurt interrupted. "Yes, it does. Rare stuff; crazy chemistry that neutralizes evil. Don't know how exactly, something to do with the pH, but it works, mostly—on the ghostly, anyway. Hey, I would have been here sooner, but it's not easy to get that many bats and spiders to spit."

"Look!" yelled Nub, pointing at Kurt's feet. Kurt Burning Trail looked down at his unusual feet. They were growing roots into the ground. Kurt snapped the roots by pulling his feet up. Nub knew that Kurt's feet would grow roots if he stood still in one place for too long.

"Well, Turner, gotta keep moving. I'll be headed into town; its time to act 'cause everything's 'out-of-whack,'" Kurt Burning Trail called out as he pulled his black bat and spider spit gun out of its holster. He lifted off the ground on his metal shoes and rode the air toward Briarwood, defying the laws of gravity. As he sped away, he said, "The Great Rain Battle has begun!"

Above Nub and his friends, the clouds tore open in a long line, following the river toward town; it began to pour in earnest.

In the downpour were hundreds more of rain people, bursting from the raindrops, running and splashing in the river: then, leaping from raindrop to raindrop as a form of transportation, they floated along in the air. This gave Nub an idea. He leaped into a raindrop, then burst out of it, landing on his feet. "We can take the raindrops into Briarwood to follow Kurt Burning Trail," Nub said. He leaped into a raindrop and floated downriver. Penny Boy jumped into one too and followed behind him.

Ready to leap into a raindrop, Nil looked around to find that the water elemental had disappeared—just like that! It had dissolved back in to the few inches of water and become part of the Yawning Rabbit River once again.

Nil called out to Jack Turner and Robert Snow, "I'm going with Nub and Penny Boy to Briarwood! White Rice, you hide here in the grasses; I'll be back for you." Nil leaped into a big raindrop and was on her way before Jack Turner or anyone else could say anything to her.

"Looks like we're next," Jack Turner said to Robert Snow.

"Us, too!" yelled the pine heads. Holding hands, Frieda and Scott leaped into a raindrop and floated downriver.

"Ridiculous pine heads," said Robert Snow. "Come on, Turner," was the last thing he said before jumping into a raindrop.

As Jack Turner was about to jump into a raindrop, he heard the hooves of horses hitting the ground; coming down the trail was Tobia and behind him was Francis Begley on Old Tom. The rest of the Begley horses—Sienna, Jimbo, and Rudy—followed.

"Francis," called out Jack Tuner, "Nub is back! He went to town with Nil and the coin-headed boy."

Francis Begley came to halt. This was great news; his son, Nil, and Penny Boy were all back safely. But it was very bad news too; the town was a war zone, and his brother, Ash, was on a murderous rampage. The smoke billowing from that direction proved it; the hospital and many houses were on fire, although the rain might help put them out, hopefully.

Knowing what he was thinking, Jack Turner added, "Kurt Burning Trail has come to help us! You see that green lightning in town?"

"Kurt Burning Trail is real?" Francis asked in astonishment. He had read the book over the years; he had enjoyed it as a boy, and he had given his copy to Penny Boy.

"Yes, very real, thankfully; he's an expert in these affairs. These are no ordinary problems," replied Jack Turner.

"Come on, let's take the horses!" Francis told Jack Turner.

White Rice and Ruby watched them ride away, down the valley road in the pouring rain—toward mayhem.

The two men on horseback, Tobia, and the other horses arrived at the edge of town, using the thick woods for cover.

From there, they caught a glimpse of the ghost hunters. Although the ghostly demons had muscular bodies, in places where the skin had rotted away, their bones showed through. They had skeleton faces and carried sharp hunting knives; swords pierced right through their bodies. Their movements were eerily fast and robotic.

As for the police of Briarwood, the six police cars were burned out. Their guns were no good to stop the ghost hunters or the molfs and only made holes in them, which made them even more vicious. The bullets could stop a cave cricket or a valley vulture, but there were so many of these creatures that it seemed pointless. Only Kurt Burning Trail's black bat– and spider-spit gun could stop the otherworldly villains by evaporating and obliterating them, but there was only one evil neutralizing gun. That was nowhere near enough; there were too many evil villains.

The ghost hunter's arrows shot into the floating raindrops and burst open the drop that carried Frieda and Scott. They fell to the ground and rolled into the street. A gnarling molf ran at them, and they quickly hid under a smoldering car. Also hiding under the car was a crying boy; it was George Melon. Frightened by the pine-headed creatures, George kicked at them to push them out from under the protection of the car and into the snarling molf's teeth. The more the pine heads tried to speak to the boy, the harder he tried to push them out.

The pine heads wanted to warn the boy that behind him, dangerously close to his jacket, was another molf. George wouldn't listen, and suddenly it was too late. The wild molf got hold of George's jacket and pulled him right out from under the car. "Ahhhhhhhhh!" George was screaming his head off and being pulled down the street in the rain—with no umbrella! However, that was the least of his problems.

Seeing what was happening, Penny Boy leaped from his raindrop and dropped to the ground. Using his metal coin head as a ram, he hit the molf that had George in its teeth. The molf squealed and released the boy. George screamed at the sight of the coin-headed boy. To protect George, Penny Boy dropped his head down again and shoved the molf as hard as he could. George ran down the street; from above, a shadow covered him. A giant valley vulture was tracking him. George, running as fast as his plump body could carry him, looked up and saw the bird's sharp talons coming closer to his head. In one swift swoop, the vulture picked up George Melon in its talons and carried the boy away as he screamed and kicked his legs.

Jack Turner and Francis Begley galloped down the main street on horseback. In the street, in the rain, were the McCarthys and the O'Sheas, fighting off the intruders as best they could, using trashcan lids as shields.

People with their umbrellas ran from their houses out into the rain screaming for help, chased by cave crickets that had broken through their basement or attic windows.

Coming toward them was the inn's owner, Frank Jones, with an arrow in his shoulder. Chef Sprinkle from the Briarwood Inn was fighting, too; he held off two cave crickets like a skilled martial artist with his kitchen knives. "You really are great," Frank Jones yelled to the chef. It seemed all his training had finally paid off.

Chief Dugan, holding an umbrella, ran by. "Turner, Begley, it's a lost cause; there's too many of them! Those who can get out of Briarwood should, now!" But honestly, it was even too late for that.

Just then, an arrow whistled through the air and hit Chief Dugan in the leg. "Uhhhhhhh," he grabbed at the arrow and fell. His leg was bleeding. A molf came at him. Francis Begley leaped from his horse onto the molf. The molf snarled and bit at him, and Francis fell off. Penny Boy charged his coin head into the molf. It screeched and ran away. Francis got up and looked at the boy. "Thank you, Penny Boy."

Penny Boy looked at Francis Begley but did not recognize him.

"Penny Boy," said Francis and went to embrace the boy, but Penny Boy was shy and backed away.

There was no time to explain. Another molf was coming at them, then another. Kurt Burning Trail suddenly appeared from behind a building and shot the molfs; they collapsed instantly.

Chief Dugan got up. His umbrella was broken, and he fumbled with it in the rain.

Jack Turner, still on horseback, now had Robert Snow on his shoulder. He called out, "Francis, Robert Snow has told me we must go to the river. Nub is there with Asheater!"

Francis leaped onto Old Tom and pulled Penny Boy up behind him, "You'll ride with me. Hold on," he told the boy, who still didn't know who this man was. They made their way through streets that were crowded with umbrella people, no-umbrella people, ghost hunters, molfs, and cave crickets—all fighting, some wounded and bleeding. Kurt Burning Trail blasted away as fast as he could, but he was vastly outnumbered.

"Drop your umbrellas!" Kurt Burning Trail shouted. "Fight together in the rain using both hands. Drop your umbrellas!"

Joe Pyeweed closed his umbrella and used it to bang a cave cricket over the head. Another person followed suit. Then, one by one, the crowd of umbrella people either dropped their umbrellas or closed them to use as weapons; they fought alongside the no-umbrella people in the pouring rain.

The ground shook under their feet. Crossing the river and coming down the main street, a massive army marched into Briarwood. It was led by Jelly Pain, the creature of dripping goo and eyeballs, as if he were a great general. Beside him were

the three pine heads, Lawrence, Diana, and Homer. Behind Jelly Pain, there were hundreds and hundreds of wild melon heads, grass goblins, stony creatures, and pine heads by the thousands. Thundering behind was the giant who had eaten the apple cake, carrying an enormous tree trunk. The giant easily stamped out the ghost hunters and cave crickets and yanked valley vultures from the sky, ignoring the piercing arrows that stuck in him.

Together, all the people of the town fought alongside this unusual army.

As Francis Begley, along with Penny Boy, Jack Turner, and Robert Snow, approached the river, he saw Asheater standing in the shallow river water; he had a hold of Nub. Nil was nowhere in sight.

Francis Begley leaped into the river. "Ash, it's me, Dusty. Leave the boy alone; let go of my son!" Francis screamed at the monster.

Nub looked at his father, astonished by what he heard. "Dad!"

Asheater's flame hand was held high, ready to strike Nub.

From the riverbank, Tobia leaped into the river and bit hard into Asheater's leg. Asheater struck at the dog, knocking him across the river; Tobia sank under the water. Penny Boy ran to the dog and pulled him out. The monster looked at Penny Boy and screeched with familiarity.

"Yes, that's Penny Boy, Ash. Ash, it's me, Dusty, your brother! Do you hear me?"

Francis moved in closer and took hold of his son. "No! Ash! Let him go, Ash, let my son go. I love him as I loved you, Ash. Ash, it's me, Dusty, your brother. Put my son down; that's my son! Ash, it's me, Dusty. Look, you didn't kill me. I'm alive, and I have a son. His name is Nub. Please put him down, Ash." He was trying so desperately to get through to his brother.

The monster looked at the man talking to him. His eyes were sullen and dark and crazed. He stared at Francis hard. Asheater straightened up and took a better look; then the monster backed away. He tried to pull the boy from Francis's grip; he couldn't, but the struggle was causing Nub pain.

"Ahhhhhhh!" Nub screamed.

Asheater swiped at Francis's face with the flaming hand, making snarling sounds.

"Uhhh!" Francis touched the burn on his face. The monster man swiped again, but Francis wouldn't let go of Nub. "I'm taking my son from you. Give Nub to me, Ash. Can you understand me? I'm Dusty, your brother!"

Francis looked down into the water, and something caught his eye. Sitting at the bottom of the river was the large sea dragon-horse tooth. He reached down and picked it up; without hesitation, he sliced at Asheater. He made a deep gash across his brother's chest, through the stained tattoo of the arrowhead. Asheater screeched like an animal. He was bleeding from the wound. Francis pulled Nub free and pushed him aside, away from the monster. Tobia ran to Nub's side and began licking his face.

Asheater was disoriented; he struck out with his flame hand, swiping in the air several times near Francis but missing him. Finally, one hit connected, and it knocked Francis down. Francis rose to his feet and with the tooth still in his hand, he came at Asheater. Again Francis slashed at Asheater with the sharp edge of the tooth; this time he cut the chain holding the medallion of Angus Gunne's arrowhead. The object fell into the water, and the water seemed to tremble.

Asheater rocked back on his feet and swayed, his dark eyes focused harder on Francis. He tried to speak, but no words came out of his mouth, just garbled sounds. He stood straight up, although it seemed to be an effort, and raised his face to the rain and the sky. He held his arms in the air. Then, suddenly, he collapsed into the river. His body went limp. The flame hand hissed and went out. All that remained was a mangled hand of charred flesh and bone. Asheater's long black hair hung in the river water. Big raindrops fell on his sickly, pale, heavily scarred face, which looked like it had its own rivers running through his skin. The river current grew stronger, and the lifeless body of Asheater began to float away downriver.

Francis reached out and caught him by the arm. He pulled the corpse back toward him against the current. Taking the dead body in his arms, Francis wept.

Penny Boy came over to Francis. He took something from his pocket and put it into Ash's mouth. It was the blue soul stone he had taken from the soul crawler in the wall of the old Miller house.

Francis watched him. "Penny Boy, what are you doing?"

Penny Boy just looked at Asheater intently, as if he expected something to happen. The scars on the monster-man's face began to fade, then disappear; his mottled skin became smooth and some living color returned. The burnt, mangled hand softened and became the normal hand of a youth. Now in Dusty's arms was the boy Ash, the brother he had known over twenty years ago. Rain fell on Ash's face, washing back his long dark hair.

The boy Ash opened his eyes and looked at his brother, then at Penny Boy. He tried to speak, "Pehhh."

"Yes! It's Penny Boy, Ash, and it's me, your brother; you didn't kill me, Ash. You can start anew, Ash," Francis told him. "With me and my family."

The boy nodded ever so little. "I will . . . I promise . . . thank you," he whispered, then closed his eyes. He died in his brother's arms, there in the river.

Francis wept again, for now he had truly lost his brother. Nub and Tobia came closer.

From behind them, the creature Jelly Pain had been watching. He climbed into the river and came over to Francis. In the town, the Great Rain Battle was over. The ghost hunters, molfs, cave crickets, and valley vultures had been no match for Jelly Pain's army and the united people of Briarwood. Jelly Pain looked down into the water and saw the arrowhead necklace that had been cut off Asheater. He picked it up.

From the woods ran Mr. Page like a crazed maniac. He raced toward the river, carrying Nil in his crushing grip. Without hesitation, and with complete accuracy, Jelly Pain threw the sharp arrowhead necklace at Mr. Page. It hit him in the head, hard. At the very same time, Kurt Burning Trail arrived and shot the creature in the head with the last of his black bat and spider spit. With that, Mr. Page's head exploded right off his body; then from head to toe, his entire being burst into pages, rather than pieces. Nil fell to the ground. She was alive. Jack Turner ran to her and picked her up. "I was looking for my turtle shell," she told him.

The pages from the green book swirled around her and fell to the ground. Penny Boy climbed out of the river and began to collect the pages and put them together.

Nub took the sea dragon-horse's tooth from his father's hand and put it in Nil's hand. "This is yours now," he said.

"Thank you, Nub," Nil said. Then she looked up. "Jelly Pain! It's you!"

"Yes, it is me granddaughter," Jelly Pain replied.

"What?" Nil was puzzled by this comment.

The rain fell on Jelly Pain. Little by little, the water washed away the goo and the dripping eyeballs until it was all gone. Underneath, there was a man, a silver-haired man in a coat of blue and gold with dark grey pants, and he wore a crown of gold and sapphires. Jelly Pain had led the army like a king, because he had once been a great king. He was King Moran, father of Daniel Moran. That made him Nil's grandfather.

In the distant past, he suffered greatly when he heard of his son's death at the hands of Angus Gunne. The king had sent the man to bring his son home, not murder him. Knowing that he was ultimately responsible for his son's death, the king suffered years of guilt and anguish. He turned slowly into the creature, a wandering lost soul full of pain. It wasn't until he met Nil, his granddaughter, by the stone circle in the pine forest that he felt a chance to live free again.

The king went over to Nil. He stroked Nil's head and kissed her cheek. There was a distinct resemblance to his son. "Daniel, your father, was my son. You saved me, little river goddess."

Nil smiled. "You saved me, too, grandfather, but . . ."

"But what?" he asked.

"Never mind, thank you," she replied. She kissed his cheek and hugged him.

"We saved each other," he added. "And now I am free to go, and you are free to be the river goddess." He touched her head where the brown fuzz was growing longer.

"Go where?" asked Nil.

"I've been in this body long enough," he said, and there was a swirl of blue wind. Where King Moran had been standing there was now a blue-and-gold kingfisher; the bird spread its splendid wings and flew away.

All along the riverbed on both sides stood the people of Briarwood. Next to them stood grass goblins, pine heads, wild melon heads, stony creatures, Robert Snow, and the four Begley horses. They had been silently watching what had been happening.

The poor giant had taken too many arrows and had sadly fallen to his death.

Kurt Burning Trail bade farewell to all of the people and creatures and his friend Jack Turner, saying that he could not stay in one place too long—as the roots growing out of his shoes proved. Also, he was out of black bat and spider spit and needed to collect more before the next out-of-the-ordinary problem arose.

Old Tom carried Ash's body to the Begley farm. That evening, in the rain, they buried him in a small meadow near the apple orchard. Jack Turner played a sweet-sounding melody on his flute as they lay the boy's body to rest.

And, as custom would have it, a young sapling was planted that very night. Dusty had selected an Ash tree in honor of his brother.

And another tree was planted that night; the townspeople dug a trench to bury the great giant, the giant who loved apple cake, near the river where he had fallen. Above his grave, they planted an apple tree sapling from the Begley farm.

Chapter Twenty-Four

A Good Start

Early the next morning, the rain continued as the river returned. Nub went to his favorite rock looking for Nil and would have gone on to Jack Turner's if she hadn't been there, but she was.

She was sitting on the rock in the rain, waiting for him. As she saw him approach, she stood up. She was smiling and radiant. "Hi, Nub." She leaped from the rock over the river to stand near him.

"Hi," said Nub. "I wondered if you would be here. Everything all right?"

"Yeah, I was just thinking about you and other things," she told him.

"Yeah, me too! What were you thinking about?"

"I was thinking about the sea dragon-horse; you know, where this tooth came from." She opened her hand to reveal the tooth.

When I was so sick, and Jelly Pain . . . eh, I mean my grandfather . . . took me into my mother's land, and I dreamed about the sea dragon-horse. I was with the her at the bottom of the sea. I looked into her open mouth and could see where the tooth was missing; the gift that she gave to my mother and me. I thought she wanted to tell me something, but she didn't say anything. I tried to ask her, but I couldn't speak. I thought I might go crazy or die right there with her. Now I think I know the answer; it's simple really, you know? I think . . . well, I *think* we're all here just to be good to one another. Just that."

Nub smiled and nodded. Then he remembered something and whispered it into her ear, "I brought you some apple cake!"

"Oh, thanks!"

As Nub slipped off his pack, Nil quietly, and without him noticing, dropped the tooth into his pocket. It was his now; she wanted him to have it.

She had just taken a bite from the apple cake when they heard voices and little footsteps coming down the path. It was Robert Snow and Ruby the fox.

"Nub! Nil! You must come with me," said the rat, a little out of breath. "The Great Watcher has awakened after all these years and has requested that you both visit him. Oh! Is that apple cake?"

"Now?" asked Nub.

"Yes, now! Grab your pack and come with me, the both of you. We must seize the moment! It's been, oh, I don't know, so long since the Great Watcher has arisen from his mountain."

"Okay, I have to go back to the farm to tell them I will be gone and get some supplies. I will be fast. Wait here for me," Nub told them.

"Okay, I'll share the cake with Robert and Ruby," Nil said.

"Yes, there's more where that came from," he called as he ran down the path.

"Mmm, that's delicious," Ruby the fox confirmed.

When Nub returned to the farm, he saw Penny Boy and Tobia out by the barn. "Penny Boy, I have to go see the Great Watcher with Nil. You stay here with Tobia and help out, please. Okay?"

Penny Boy's eyes got huge thinking about the Great Watcher, but he nodded his understanding. Tobia understood as well; he would stay with Penny Boy on the farm.

"I'll leave a note on the table for Mom and Dad," Nub called out on his way to the back door.

Nub returned to the river where Nil, Robert Snow, and Ruby were waiting for him.

"Okay, I've got some things; let's go!"

"If we hurry, we can be there in two days," Robert Snow said, sitting on the back of Nub's pack. Ruby the fox was walking next to Nil. White Rice was safe and sound back at Jack Turner's house.

When they arrived a couple of days later, Nub and Nil approached the steep slope.

"I'll wait here for you both," Robert Snow announced, standing by the pine forest at the base of the mountain where the river ran. "It's better if you go on your own."

Nub and Nil climbed the grassy slope. There, sitting at the top of it, was the giant sheep-man, waiting for them. To Nub's surprise, sheep were grazing where none had been before. This time, though, there were no vicious molfs chasing them, as Sean had experienced. The Great Watcher's fiery, dark eyes watched as the pair approached him.

The Great Watcher's first comment was surprisingly light-hearted and ordinary. "I smell apple cake," he said.

Nub laughed. "Yes, I have a piece in my pack. Would you like it?"

The Great Watcher smiled at this generous offer. "No, thank you." He bowed his head to Nub and Nil. "You both have done well." The Great Watcher took a wooden stick from the ground and touched it to Nub's arm. With a flash of electricity, Nub felt a burn, and there on his arm was the tattoo of the Great Watcher. Then the Watcher did the same to Nil's arm but with a flash of fire.

Nub looked at the mark on her arm. "Look!" he exclaimed.

Nil turned her arm and smiled to see a turtle shell with markings just like her old shell. "Thank you," whispered Nil.

"You're welcome." The Great Watcher paused, then spoke with sparkling eyes, "Speaking of apple cake, it must be exceptional; it awoke a giant from a spell. I know he fought for your people and for the river and gave his life for them. He has honored all the giants and has undone the curse."

"I have an idea," Nub said excitedly. "I have some apples from our orchard in my pack. If I leave them with you, you could give them to the giants; they could grow their own apple trees and have orchards here in the valley, and maybe even learn to make apple cake!"

Nub took off his pack and left the four golden pippin apples on the ground near him. "It would be a good start," the boy said.

"Yes, it would be a good start," agreed the Great Watcher.

Nub and Nil watched the sheep-man close his big, dark eyes; the ground rumbled as he sank back into the earth and became the top of the mountain. Where he had been, only the four yellow apples, rocks, dirt, moss, and grass remained.

The rain continued steadily for another two weeks. In the town of Briarwood, some people still used umbrellas but more people didn't; that was fine, it made no difference anymore. The Yawning Rabbit River was full again and ran stronger than ever. Jumping Grace Falls fell into the clear pool below where a new golden carp swam.

Winter came to the Briarwood Forest, and the rain turned to snow. The forest was quiet under the white blanket. In Jack Turner's house, by the fire, Robert Snow and Jack Turner carefully put together the old green book, page by page.

The following spring, the tender, bright-green leaves returned to the bare Briarwood Forest; and, thanks to the reckless and hungry pine heads, who had opened the metal box full of rose seeds and spilled them, the Great Forest blossomed with golden Penny roses during the first weeks of June.

It was the most beautiful summer that Nub and Nil could remember.

Penny Boy and Tobia, Robert Snow and Ruby often found Nub and Nil by the river; they had summer picnics among the roses and bluebells that grew there.

The great-blue heron would usually sit nearby, and it seemed to come even closer when Robert Snow was telling his stories of the Yawning Rabbit River.

Above them, watching over the river from tree branches, was the crested kingfisher whom Nil named Grandfather.

One fall day, just when the apples and pumpkins were ready to pick, a most auspicious announcement was placed in the *Briarwood Times:* "Frances and Gina Begley are happy to announce the birth of their twin babies, Sean and Violet Begley. Brother and sister to Nub and Penny Boy. Congratulations to them all."